# ENTRUSTED

## CLUB DESTINY

**AUSTIN ARROWS**
Rush
Kaufman

**CLUB DESTINY**
Conviction
Temptation
Addicted
Seduction
Infatuation
Captivated
Devotion
Perception
Entrusted
Adored
Distraction

**DEAD HEAT RANCH**
Boots Optional
Betting on Grace
Overnight Love

**DEVIL'S BEND**
Chasing Dreams
Vanishing Dreams

**MISPLACED HALOS**
Protected in Darkness
Salvation in Darkness
Bound in Darkness

**OFFICE INTRIGUE**
Office Intrigue
Intrigued Out of The Office
Their Rebellious Submissive
Their Famous Dominant
Their Ruthless Sadist
Their Naughty Student
Their Fairy Princess
Owned

**PIER 70**
Reckless
Fearless
Speechless
Harmless
Clueless

**SNIPER 1 SECURITY**
Wait for Morning
Never Say Never
Tomorrow's Too Late

**SOUTHERN BOY MAFIA/DEVIL'S PLAYGROUND**
Beautifully Brutal
Without Regret
Beautifully Loyal
Without Restraint

**STANDALONE NOVELS**
Unhinged Trilogy
A Million Tiny Pieces
Inked on Paper
Bad Reputation
Bad Business

**NAUGHTY HOLIDAY EDITIONS**
2015
2016

# ENTRUSTED

## CLUB DESTINY

# NICOLE EDWARDS

## NICOLE EDWARDS LIMITED

A dba of SL Independent Publishing, LLC
PO Box 1086
Pflugerville, Texas 78691

---

### ENTRUSTED
Club Destiny, 9
Nicole Edwards

---

COVER DETAILS:

Image: © Branislav Ostojic | Dreamstime.com; © Frugo | 123rf.com
Design: © Nicole Edwards Limited

INTERIOR DETAILS:

Formatting: Nicole Edwards Limited
Editing: Blue Otter Editing | www.BlueOtterEditing.com

IDENTIFIERS:

ISBN: (ebook) 978-1-939786-22-7 | (paperback) 978-1-939786-21-0

BISAC: FICTION / Romance / General

Dear Keith,

Although we have never actually met, I wanted to let you know that you have changed my life in inexplicable ways. In ways that I never imagined possible.

Some might say that it was a mutual love of books that introduced me to your sister, Denise. I, however, believe that you had a hand in that introduction. You, a man who suffered in a way so many people still don't understand, brought us together for reasons far greater.

Thanks to your family's courage and strength, so many of us have learned your story. And through your story and those who have stories similar, we are learning that there are options, there is help. Mental illness is still misunderstood by so many, but there are people who understand the darkness is real, and it needs attention.

It wasn't until recently that I was able to share my own story about my battle with depression. This, my friend, is something that I am forever grateful to you for. You have made me stronger.

So, from your perch high above us all, as you look down upon us, I hope you can see all of the lives you've affected, all of the people you have helped, and all of the love that has been reserved just for you.

~Nicole


For those of you who would like to learn more about Keith Milano's story, you can do so at www.KeithMilano.org

# PROLOGUE

*Sunday evening, at Devotion...*

SAMANTHA MCCOY WAS ROOTED TO THE FLOOR.

As she stood outside of one of the occupied glass rooms that acted as a center stage at Devotion, she was focused intently on Mistress Serena and the sexy scene playing out in front of her.

The scene was relatively similar to the one she'd witnessed between Xander and Mercedes last week during their first night at Devotion. At least as far as setup went. Similar to the way Xander had structured his scene, Mistress Serena was using a St. Andrew's cross, a flogger, and sheer determination to command the scantily clad male subs currently occupying the space.

But that's about where the similarities ended.

The biggest difference was that Sam had witnessed more than just domination between Xander and Mercedes. Even with her inexperienced eye, she'd caught on to the fact that there was an inferno of emotion raging between the two of them.

With Mistress Serena, her scenes lacked that emotional connection, although they were a little more intimate when she was playing with one or both of her own subs. As she was now.

No, what Mistress Serena offered to the audience was always about hard-core, erotic exchanges. And the majority of the time, she interacted with the members, taking them on and teaching them through participation just what it meant to submit to a Domme.

Sam hadn't considered the differences before, but Xander had certainly made her realize the true depth of emotion that could be shared between a Dominant and a submissive. Until she had seen it with her own two eyes, she hadn't thought anything of it.

Not that it mattered. Based on what she remembered of the scene, Mercedes had enjoyed herself on both occasions. Just like the dark-haired man in the glass room facing the audience was. Even strapped to the cross, he seemed to be having just as much fun. As was the blond man bent over in front of him, currently sucking the other man's cock while Mistress Serena impaled Blondie with a large black dildo.

Clearly, based on the sensual cries echoing from the room, Mistress Serena was doing something right.

While Sam could only see one man's face, she could hear the need in both of their combined moans. Whatever they were feeling, it was undeniably gratifying, and it sent a punch of pleasure through Sam. Almost like she was experiencing it vicariously through them.

"Oh," Samantha mumbled when the blond man writhed and moaned loudly, his voice echoing through the enclosed room.

The heat of a body moved up against her, and Sam instantly recognized it was Logan. Even if she had been blindfolded, she would've been able to tell it was him. As she leaned into him, he banded his arms around her and rested his hands on her stomach. His rigid erection was pressed into her back, proof that he was enjoying the scene as much as she was.

Then again, it was easy to enjoy it when you were on the outside looking in. It was somewhat like porn, only significantly better. It was exciting to watch as the provocatively dressed Mistress Serena pleasured both of her subs in a way only she could obviously do.

The woman knew how to play them like a finely tuned instrument. She didn't hesitate as she continued to land several smacks on the blond's rosy red ass while she fucked his ass with a thick dildo repeatedly.

From where Sam stood, she could see the tension in the blond guy's muscles, the pure pleasure in the dark-haired man's eyes. The restrained man looked as though he were damn close to exploding. Knowing Mistress Serena, she'd refused her subs the pleasure. At least until she gave them permission.

"Enjoying yourself?" Logan asked, his breath warm against her neck.

"It's entertaining, yes," she said, turning her head to look up at him. "How about you?"

"I can't complain."

Sam turned her attention back to the scene. Logan had been across the room talking to a handsome man she hadn't recognized while she'd been chatting with Sierra shortly after they'd arrived. When Luke and Cole had come to retrieve their wife, Sam had originally intended to join Logan, but then she'd been distracted by Mistress Serena.

"Who were you talking to?" she asked him now, resting her hands atop his where they were wrapped around her.

"Someone I'd like to introduce you to."

"Yeah?" Sam was still focused on the scene in front of her. The blond man being fucked ruthlessly was moaning in earnest, obviously dangerously close to orgasm.

"Later, though. Right now, I'm not sure how much more of this I can take," Logan breathed against her ear. "I need to be inside you."

Sam turned abruptly, no longer interested in what was going on with Mistress Serena and her play toys. They were quite capable of handling themselves. Right now, more than anything, Sam wanted Logan.

"Where?" she asked, looking away long enough to see what was going on around them.

"I've got a room," he told her, but Sam could see he was about to elaborate. She didn't say a word. "I've reserved a room upstairs that has a swing similar to that one," he told her, motioning toward the sex swing that had been set up on the main floor.

Sam had heard rumors that the sex swing had been a huge hit on the club's first theme night. So much so, they were apparently going to keep it as a nightly attraction for now.

Sam sucked in a sharp breath as realization dawned, her eyes slamming back to his.

A swing? Was he serious?

Excitement had her stomach bottoming out. They were really going to do this. Experiment with BDSM. Just the two of them. She fought the urge to turn back to Mistress Serena's scene. There was no way it would be like that, would it?

She was suddenly grateful Logan had opted to make tonight private. It was one thing to try something new. It was something entirely different to do it in front of so many inquisitive eyes.

Looking around again, she took stock of what was happening around her. She had been so engrossed in Mistress Serena's scene that she hadn't even noticed that there were quite a few more people than when they had arrived a short while ago.

There was a couple, right at that very moment, getting it on on one of the couches. The woman was leaning over the back of the couch while one man was plowing her from behind. Another man was sitting on the couch, teasing the woman's breasts and kissing her in the process. No wasting time for those three.

The sight sent a shiver of anticipation through Sam.

Her attention strayed, and she found her gaze transfixed on Luke, Cole, and Sierra. More specifically, Cole. On his knees, sucking Luke into his mouth while Sierra stood behind him, her hands sliding through his blond hair.

God, that was hot.

So fucking hot.

Not that she ever wanted another man to touch Logan or vice versa, but to watch Luke and Cole... It was erotic.

Logan must've noticed what she was looking at because once again he was talking, leaning in close to her ear. "Is there something else you'd prefer to be doing?"

*I want a threesome*, she wanted to say, but she didn't. It was the truth, though, and the desire was hammered home by the fact that there were quite a few threesomes going on around her at that moment.

Like a sign. One that taunted her with something she couldn't have.

A threesome with her husband and another man was what she wanted, and she knew there was no way to deny it at this point. However, tonight was about experimenting with something they hadn't done before. Something that might possibly take her mind off the threesomes.

Not likely, but whatever.

"No, the swing sounds like fun," she finally told him.

She needed to come to terms with the fact that there wouldn't be a third in their future. Since neither she nor Logan was looking for a permanent third, and there was no way to get a man to commit to forever without getting something more than sex out of the deal, she had to accept there would be no positive outcome.

She and Logan wanted two different things when it came to a polyamorous relationship. She knew that.

Logan took her hand and she allowed him to lead her toward the stairs. She followed as he ascended to the second floor and then directed her down the narrow hall that overlooked the main floor. One last glance over to Luke, Cole, and Sierra before Sam swallowed hard and accepted her fate.

A threesome wasn't in the cards for her.

She did her best to hide her disappointment.

"Do you want me to make sure no one comes in?" Logan asked as they stepped inside the small room.

Sam stopped in the center of the room, ignoring the bright white walls and the row of matching cabinets on one side, choosing instead to look at the swing hanging from a steel beam overhead.

Okay, now this looked interesting.

All thoughts of threesomes disappearing, Sam's body reignited at the thought of what Logan was about to do to her.

"No," she told him without turning back to look at him. The fact that someone could watch them was part of the excitement.

Logan made his way over to her, pressing his front to her back, his cock still stiff between them. When his hands caressed her shoulders, his fingers sliding beneath the thin straps of her dress, Sam closed her eyes as he easily slid them down her arms.

Within seconds, Logan had worked the dress down her body, the silk pooling at her feet, while the cool air in the small room immediately tickled her skin.

Okay, so they weren't going to waste any time. That was completely fine with her. As it was, Logan's mere presence made her body burn, her lust coalescing into turbulent, driving need.

Well, his presence and the wild ideas running through her head about what they'd be doing in that swing.

"Damn, baby. Do you know how fucking hot you make me?"

"*Me?*" she asked, putting her hands over his when he cupped her naked breasts, kneading them firmly. "I thought you were turned on by watching Mistress Serena."

"I was turned on by thinking about fucking you in this swing. Watching your naked body as I drive my cock deep in your pussy. It fucking turns me on, Sam."

Well, when he put it that way…

Sam inhaled when he began to tweak her nipples between his forefingers and thumbs. Allowing her head to drop back against his chest, she gave in to the sensations consuming her.

"Is that what you want, Sam? For me to drive my cock deep in your pussy?"

"Yes," she moaned as he continued to drive her crazy with just his hands.

He leaned down, his fingers pinching and pulling her nipples while his warm breath caressed her cheek. "Nice and deep," he groaned softly. "I'll slide into your slick heat while you rock in the swing, impaling yourself on my dick."

Sam moaned. She loved when he talked like that.

"Are you ready for me to strap you in?"

Eyeing the swing, she tried to figure out just how it functioned. Wow. That was one seriously strange-looking contraption. From what she could tell, there was a padded strap for her to sit on, one that would support her lower back, and then one for her neck.

Interesting.

There were also what appeared to be ankle and wrist restraints attached, and though Sam couldn't quite picture exactly how that would work, her body heated nicely at the thought of being completely restrained for Logan.

"I'm ready."

"Turn around," Logan whispered, his hands on her waist.

Sam turned to face him and then Logan took care of the rest. The next thing she knew, she was resting somewhat comfortably — although entirely naked — in the swing.

"Damn," Logan mumbled beneath his breath. "You look so much better than I even imagined. And trust me; I've been hot and bothered just from my imagination. You. Here. So much better. Fuck."

Sam watched longingly as Logan unbuttoned and unzipped his slacks, freeing his thick, heavy cock. With unabashed interest, she continued to admire him while he stroked himself slowly, his gaze raking over her from head to foot, lingering at a few places in between.

"What are you waiting for?" she asked, her eyes darting up to meet his. Nothing like taunting Logan when he looked at her with so much fire in his eyes.

She loved watching him lose control, and clearly, this was one of those times when he was going to do just that.

"NOT A DAMN THING," LOGAN SAID, ANSWERING his sassy wife's question.

He honestly wasn't waiting for anything, unless holding himself in check was a valid reason for him to be stalling.

Logan was doing his best to control himself, but seeing his wife spread out in that swing, all of the images going through his mind of what it would be like to fuck her while she was suspended in midair... Yeah, well, needless to say, he wasn't going to last forever.

His cock was throbbing, his balls aching, and he was ready to feel the silky wet depths of her pussy wrapped around him. Hell, he'd been ready since the moment she'd stepped out of their bedroom wearing that sexy black dress that he knew she loved.

Moving forward, because frankly he couldn't take it anymore, Logan made a couple of minor adjustments to the swing, using the levers to hoist Sam up to the right height for him to slide right into her.

Ahh, God. The thought of his cock tunneling into her, her pussy milking him, pulling him in deep while he pounded away at her...

"Fuck, baby," he growled. "Stroke my cock," he told her gruffly as he stepped around to the side, feeling his control slipping a little more with each passing second. "Slow and easy."

If she did anything else, he might just go off in her hand.

While Sam teased him with her soft, smooth fingers along his shaft, Logan took the time to restrain her legs, lifting them up and open so that she wouldn't have to do any of the work. When he was finished, she was relaxing back on the narrow straps, her legs forming a wide V, leaving her open and waiting for him.

Taking over stroking — which didn't feel nearly as good as when she did it — Logan made his way between her thighs once more.

Unable to resist, Logan dropped to one knee between Sam's creamy thighs and drove his tongue deep into her warm, wet heat.

"Oh, shit," she moaned, and he felt the swing rock as she reached for his head, firmly latching on to his hair.

Gripping the straps to keep her in place, Logan teased her with his mouth, alternating between fucking her with his tongue and tormenting her clit. When Sam was begging and pleading, attempting to thrust against his mouth, Logan stood and, without pause, drove his cock inside her.

"Logan!" Sam moaned passionately, her head falling back.

Logan held his breath as the vicelike grip of her cunt hugged his cock, clamping down rigorously as he thrust deeper until he was fully seated inside of her.

"So fucking sexy," he told Sam, smiling down at her while he held tight to the nylon straps suspending her from the ceiling. "I'm going to get one of these for the house."

Sam smiled up at him, her hips undulating as though she might actually be able to control the swing. Logan held firm, not allowing her to move.

"You feel so good," he told her.

"Not as good as you," she moaned again. "Please, Logan! Fuck me!"

"My pleasure, baby."

With slow, rhythmic movements, Logan put the swing in motion. As he pushed gradually on the straps, his cock pulled out of her until only the head was inside. And when he pulled her back toward him, using the momentum of the swing, he thrust his hips forward, driving himself into her.

He wasn't sure how he managed to keep his legs from going out from beneath him, but long minutes passed as he continued to maintain a steady pace, unwilling to go too fast because she felt so fucking good.

Logan was just about to increase the tempo when Sam's attention moved toward the door. Without looking behind him, Logan felt the presence of another person. When Sam's eyes darted up toward him and then back to the person, Logan knew exactly who was there. Even if Sam didn't know who he was.

Natural possessive instincts kicked in, putting Logan on alert. He was all for Elijah Penn watching them — it was part of Logan's overall plan for the evening; however, because this was their first interaction, he wouldn't allow Elijah to get too close.

Wanting to pull Sam's attention back to him, Logan began to increase his tempo, driving into her as he jerked the swing back at him, lodging him deep. "So tight, baby. I want to feel you come on my cock. Can you do that?"

"Yes," she whispered, her eyes locked with his once more.

Logan could see the interest, the obvious arousal from the added audience, but he refused to let his attention stray. At least for now.

"Do you want it fast and hard? Or slow and easy?" he asked Sam, knowing he was going to be pushing his luck if she went with the latter.

"Slow. And deep. God, it feels so good."

Sam's breaths were labored as he continued to thrust into her, fighting to maintain a steady pace, but as more time passed, as his balls drew up to his body, Logan knew it was only a matter of time before he was going to lose it.

Sam's eyes averted once more, and that's when Logan noticed Elijah moving into his peripheral vision. As he had been the last time Logan had seen him, Elijah was nicely dressed, his black slacks and jacket contrasting with the white shirt he wore. The man looked like he'd just stepped off the pages of a fashion magazine as far as Logan was concerned — but, oddly enough, he also didn't look like the type of guy who would walk in on them like this.

No, Elijah looked like the type of guy who would be at the helm of a situation such as this, commanding the interaction, pulling the strings.

Just because he looked like a man who wanted to be in control didn't necessarily mean that he was. Logan already knew what Elijah was looking for.

Another part of the plan.

"Your wife is very beautiful," Elijah said with only a hint of an accent.

Logan didn't respond. At least not to Elijah's statement.

"What do you want me to do, Sam?" Logan asked, focusing his full attention on his wife. This was exactly how Logan had intended tonight to go.

Logan knew Sam. He knew that she was mollifying him with her agreement to try out BDSM. Although Xander might've thought this would deter Sam from wanting a threesome, Logan had known better. And the way she was watching Elijah confirmed his suspicions. This was what she wanted.

As far as he was concerned, the swing was indeed the type of bondage he could get on board with, so he wasn't opposed to experimenting from time to time. But he had also come to the conclusion that the type of interaction he'd seen between Xander and Mercedes just wasn't for him. He could bring himself to spank Sam on occasion — with his hand — but anything else was out of the question. It just didn't do it for him. Granted, he might find a few other BDSM-related activities they could try, but he wasn't sure it was even necessary.

Logan had the feeling Sam was still more interested in a threesome. He knew *he* definitely was.

"Fuck me," she said on a breathless moan, her eyes transfixed on their visitor. "Fuck me hard, Logan."

"You like being watched?" Elijah asked, and Logan noticed Sam's eyes flare with what was unquestionably heat. His wife did like an audience. More importantly, she liked the concept of a threesome.

"Yes," she responded, the single word punctuated by Logan's thrust.

"Then I'll watch," Elijah confirmed, his hands in his pockets as he stood casually by.

Logan could no longer wait. Elijah's presence, his eyes on Sam's gloriously naked body while she was being fucked, was more than he could stand.

"Look at me, Sam," Logan ordered.

Her eyes moved to his quickly, a radiant smile breaking out on her face.

"Hard and fast." It wasn't a question, but he said the words anyway.

"Yes, please."

"When you come, I want to hear my name on your lips," he told her, his voice steady as he increased the pace of his thrusts.

It could've been a minute, it could've been ten, hell, Logan had no idea, but when Sam screamed his name, her pussy gripping him like a velvet fist, Logan lost all control. He slammed into her once, twice, three more times before he came violently, his thighs trembling from the intensity.

Logan made quick work of cleaning himself up, tucking his spent cock back into his slacks, and then tending to Sam gently. After helping her out of the swing and assisting her back into her dress, Logan turned around to introduce Sam to...

No one.

Elijah was gone.

# CHAPTER ONE

*The next day...*

ELIJAH PENN HIT THE END BUTTON ON his cell phone and then clutched it in his hand as he slipped into his Acura RLX waiting patiently for him in the downtown Dallas parking garage of Virtual Impact, Inc.

He'd just finished a conference call with one of the sales managers in VI's Singapore office and had managed to sneak out of the building before another fire could erupt. Considering it was early Tuesday morning on the other side of the globe, he knew if he were to stick around much longer, the likelihood of someone demanding his attention in the very near future grew exponentially.

Elijah dropped his phone into the cup holder and then started the car, buckling his seat belt as he stared out into the darkness of the parking garage. Shit. As with most days that he left the office — when he was actually *in* the office — it was already dark outside, and that did little to improve his mood.

He was feeling a little burned out, and the sad thing was that it was only Monday. After a solid twelve hours in the office, he was finally leaving, the conference call tying up the last of the pressing issues he'd encountered upon his arrival that morning. The day had seemed never-ending.

It didn't help that he'd spent most of the past weekend in their newly constructed offices in Florida, assisting their director of sales with getting things set up. While he'd been doing that, another weekend had come and gone.

Of course, working twenty-four/seven was his fault entirely. His life now revolved around work. And there was no one to blame but himself.

Rather than head home when his plane had returned him safely to Texas yesterday afternoon, Elijah had made the mistake of going into the office. After spending several hours on the phone — on a Sunday — Elijah had finally had enough. His overdue bout with frustration had led him to Devotion and ultimately to meeting — although not officially — Samantha McCoy.

Fuck. The memory of what he'd seen last night jolted him, at once reviving his mood.

After the day he'd just had, part of him wanted to head home and call it a night. The other part of him was interested in something else entirely.

Then again, he wasn't up to being alone at the moment.

Not tonight.

Rather than dwell on going home to a cold, lonely house, he opted to look on the bright side. It wasn't an easy task for him, but he'd been attempting to do just that for the last few years.

The first positive: he should've been on another airplane, several hours into a twenty-hour flight, but luckily, the spur-of-the-moment trip that would've taken him out of the country that morning had been cancelled at the last minute.

Being that he was a senior director for the global sales division of Virtual Impact, Inc., an industry leader in storage and server virtualization, Elijah was used to odd hours, impromptu trips out of the country, and yes, plenty of high drama.

For whatever reason, he had been granted a reprieve. At least for today. Which meant tonight, he was looking to go off the grid for a few hours. And yes, he had a place in mind.

Tomorrow would be here soon enough, so tonight, he had plans. Another thing to look forward to.

He was pulling out of the parking garage and onto the dark, narrow road that would take him to the highway when his cell phone rang.

His car's Bluetooth read off the number, and he hit the talk button as soon as he recognized it. "Hello," he greeted.

"I got your message," Logan McCoy said, forgoing any pleasantries. Elijah was quite used to the American custom of getting right to the point by now, so it didn't bother him.

"Thanks for calling me back," Elijah said, his attention on the road in front of him. "Apologizing to your voice mail seemed inappropriate."

"Apologize?"

"Yeah. For disappearing on you last night," Elijah stated bluntly. There was no need to beat around the bush; Elijah knew as well as Logan that his disappearance after that scene had been rude.

"What the fuck happened?" Logan asked, just as brusquely.

He'd lost his nerve, that's what had happened. He had seen Samantha McCoy for the first time, and he'd been at a loss. It had nothing to do with the fact that she'd been restrained in a swing, being fucked into oblivion by her husband, either. It had been what he'd seen in her eyes that had blindsided him.

"I fucked up," he told Logan now, going for the truth.

"I took your disappearance to mean you weren't interested."

"Oh, I'm interested." Elijah sighed heavily. A little too much.

"Funny way of showing it."

"Again, I apologize. I just... I hadn't expected that."

"What? To find me fucking my wife?"

Elijah laughed, without an ounce of humor. There had been nothing remotely funny about what he'd witnessed last night. It had been intense, but not at all humorous.

"Explain it to me, Penn. The last thing I'm interested in is having my wife hurt. Do you understand me?"

"Loud and clear," Elijah answered candidly. "I have no excuse. I ... panicked. But I'd like to apologize to Samantha. Tonight."

Logan's heavy sigh gave Elijah a smidgen of hope. He was the first to admit that second chances were tough to come by.

"Yeah, you mentioned you were going to Devotion tonight," Logan retorted.

Elijah had mentioned it on the voice mail he'd left Logan early that morning. It was an attempt to make amends for being a coward last night.

"Does this mean that I'll see you and Samantha tonight?" Elijah asked.

"You will." Logan's voice was firm and confident, but Elijah heard something else in the man's tone.

"But?" he encouraged, waiting patiently for what was to come.

"I'm not putting her through that again. You need to figure out if this is what you want before you show up." There was a brief pause before Logan continued. "As it was, Sam asked about you. She'd seen us talking earlier in the evening. She's not stupid, Elijah. She knew I had something planned."

Elijah had met Logan last week during his first visit to X-hale, an upscale cigar bar owned by Xander Boone. An off-the-cuff invitation from Trent Ramsey, a man Elijah had known for many years after having met him in a hotel bar of all places, had sparked Elijah's interest. It went without saying that Elijah had been curious enough to attend.

"Understood. I'd very much like to meet her," Elijah said through clenched teeth. He could own up to his mistakes and even handle a dressing down when necessary, but it wasn't easy. He had to remind himself that Logan had a damn good reason for being pissed off.

"We'll be heading that direction in about an hour and a half," Logan finally said. "I'll need to give Sam time to get ready."

"I'll find you when I get there," Elijah informed him casually. "If you're busy, I'll wait."

"I'll keep my eye out for you. Oh, and Elijah" — Logan lowered his voice — "don't fuck this up again."

With that, the call ended.

Although they had never met face-to-face until last week, Elijah had heard of Logan McCoy. According to Logan, the rumor mill ran both ways, especially in their industry. In fact, XTX was a very loyal customer and Logan's name was mentioned frequently when it came to their business. However, Elijah had not been privy to the sort of information he had learned about the highly respected man after their first introduction. And the info he had obtained wasn't just rumor or speculation.

It'd come straight from the horse's mouth, so to speak.

After Xander had called Elijah out about his preference for threesomes that night, Elijah had shared a different sort of conversation with Logan.

*After* they had left X-hale.

It had been quite interesting, and truthfully, it had left Elijah anticipating their next chance encounter. He hadn't expected to see Logan and Samantha so soon after that conversation, but his change of plans on Sunday had prompted him to contact Logan rather than put it off.

He had been given a chance at something he was certainly interested in, and he had failed. Knowing Logan's reputation, Elijah hadn't actually expected a second chance after he had disappeared on them last night. When he'd woken up that morning, he had thought he had some time to think it through before he contacted Logan again.

Then he'd found out that his next trip had been cancelled.

The moment he'd learned about his change of plans, Elijah had manned up and placed the call. Unfortunately, he had been greeted by Logan's voice mail. He wasn't quite sure what to expect from Logan, or if the man would even call him back, but now that Elijah had apologized, he felt a measure of relief.

When he pulled into his driveway several minutes later, he didn't bother glancing around at the exterior of his single-story brick house. He knew what he would find if he did. The yard was immaculate, the shrubbery and the grass kept trimmed and neat. There were several trees and well-placed lights along the driveway, and that was usually all he noticed, if even that. Elijah paid a company to maintain his yard weekly, mainly because he didn't care enough to deal with it.

If life hadn't been so incredibly cruel, Elijah would've been coming home to his wife. But that hadn't been the case for the last four years because Beth was dead. His beautiful, vivacious wife had died after a long, brutal battle with cancer, leaving him with a heavy heart that still beat with her memory.

Had Beth still been alive, she would have insisted that they maintain the yard themselves. Then again, if Beth were still alive, the gardens around the house would've been brimming with bright flowers that she would've planted herself and Elijah would've been home long before dark, business be damned.

But he was coming home to an empty house. Just like he had each and every night for the last four years.

Once he was parked alongside the garage, he shut off the engine and stared out into the night. He glanced over at the garage door as he sat there. He could have parked inside the garage, but that would have meant he needed to remove the multitude of boxes that still remained there. Rows of cardboard stacked on the cold concrete, collecting dust after all these years.

The boxes were full of Beth's things. The things his mother and his sister had helped him to pack up just two years ago in an attempt to help him move forward. Not move on, because they all knew that would never happen.

He hadn't thought it possible, but it had helped. A little.

Taking a deep breath, he opened the door, climbed out of his car, and then headed into the house.

Elijah yanked at his tie as he made his way through the dimly lit rooms, ignoring everything around him. The inside was much like the outside. It was maintained by someone he paid to keep it clean and dust free. Aside from the furniture, the only things to remind him of his beautiful wife were pictures that lined the mantel on the fireplace that was never used. Other than that, the place was cold. Sterile.

Nothing like the home he'd had when Beth had been alive.

Habit had him twisting his wedding band around and around on his finger as he made his way to the bathroom.

Although Beth had been gone for years, Elijah still missed her. Terribly. He thought about her all the time, and yes, he even talked to her. Talking to her made him feel better. It was the fact that she couldn't talk back that hurt so much.

Beth had pleaded with him for months before she died, begging him to go on with his life once she was gone, to find someone who would make him happy. Someone he could love.

*"I need to know that you'll take care of yourself,"* Beth said *through a watery smile. Elijah knew she held her tears at bay because of him. She was so damn brave it broke his heart.*

*"I'll keep moving along,"* he told her, squeezing her hand gently. *"I can promise you that."*

*"Promise me that you'll find a way to be happy,"* Beth had rasped. *"I don't want to leave you all alone."*

*"I won't be alone,"* he lied.

*"I know that,"* she told him. *"You've got your family. They'll take good care of you. But that's not what I mean, and you know it. You're young, Eli. You deserve to be happy. You deserve to find someone who will love you as much as I do."*

*"I don't want anyone else,"* he told her, the tears that he fought so hard to keep from her breaking free. *"I don't need anyone else, Beth. You're it for me."*

What Beth had not understood was that there wasn't enough room in his heart for anyone else, and Elijah feared there never would be. Beth was all he wanted. All he needed. Even if he only had her memory now.

Elijah would have said he would give anything to have her back, but he still remembered the last two years of her life. The terrible suffering that she'd endured while she and the doctors did everything in their power to beat the cancer that had eaten away at her brain.

He would never want that for her again, and ultimately, he knew she was in a much better place. To want her to have to suffer just so he could have her with him would've been selfish.

And that was one thing Elijah wasn't.

As far as he was concerned, he had already experienced the greatest pleasure that life had to offer. He was married to the most wonderful woman to grace the planet. And yes, he still considered them married. They would be until the day he died and went to join her.

Until then, Elijah just had to keep on moving along. Just like he'd told Beth he would. And tonight, he fully intended to look forward to what the future might hold. Because until he could be with Beth again, he knew he had to do what was necessary to be as happy as he could be.

After all, he had made a promise to Beth.

# CHAPTER TWO

SAMANTHA SPENT MORE TIME GETTING READY THAN she knew was necessary, but no amount of talking to herself had seemed to calm her.

She was ... antsy.

Yes, antsy. That was probably the best word to describe the way she had been feeling for the last hour. Her restlessness seemed to be brought on by a mixture of nerves and anticipation. Mixed with a minuscule amount of confusion and uncertainty.

In a word, she was a mess.

A short while ago, after she and Logan had finished dinner, as Sam was cleaning the kitchen, Logan had excused himself to make a call. Sam had instantly assumed the call was work related. When he'd come back into the kitchen to tell her he wanted to take her to Devotion again tonight, she'd realized he hadn't been talking business.

At first, she'd been confused. They had just gone the night before, and going several days in a row generally wasn't his MO.

Rather than question Logan's sudden interest in going again, Sam had immediately acquiesced. Especially after she'd noticed the hunger that had returned to his eyes.

Whoever had been on the other end of that call had brought about the spontaneous request to go to the club, and that intrigued her.

Sam had a feeling it was the dark-haired man with the golden eyes from the night before. The man who Logan had seemed to want to introduce her to, but who had disappeared before that opportunity had arisen. Her gut was telling her that Logan hadn't just come up with the plan on his own. Sure, they were frequent visitors to the club — first Club Destiny, now Devotion — but not like this. Not as a nightly ritual.

To be honest, Sam hadn't expected to go back to Devotion at all. At least not for a while. Not after the conversation she and Logan had shared on the drive in to the office last Wednesday.

*"Are you interested in what you saw last night, baby?"* Logan asked.

*"Are you referring to the watching? Or are you asking if I'd like to try something like that?"* she asked.

*"Participating."*

*Sam wasn't sure how to explain herself. She was so confused about what was going on that she had a hard time putting all of the pieces together herself, much less coming up with a way to discuss it with Logan. She really needed more answers from him before she could put words to what she was feeling. She simply said, "I think it would be interesting to try."*

*"Interesting?"*

*Sam didn't answer him. She didn't know what to say, so she just waited him out, hoping they could change the subject. At least until she could get her thoughts together.*

*"Is this BDSM stuff something* you're *interested in?"* she finally asked when they were halfway to the office.

*"Depends. I could be persuaded into trying."*

Sam turned to face him more fully. He sounded as though he would need as much, if not more, encouragement as she would to move forward with it. It only added to her confusion. "I don't know what I want anymore."

"Talk to me, Sam."

God, she was frustrated. And confused. She felt as though Logan was trying to coax her into wanting the BDSM stuff, but she wasn't convinced that he was really all that into it. Which didn't make sense.

"I don't even know how to explain it."

"Baby, you're gonna have to try. This is your show. If you want to try something new, I need to know what it is."

"You're not interested in asking Xander to be...?"

"No. I don't think Xander is the right person. But I won't deny that I thought about it."

Clearly, he had known exactly what she was referring to.

"I had, too." She had actually been excited by the idea of a threesome.

Sam watched the road in front of them for a moment before she asked, "Do you think Xander would be willing to help us with this BDSM stuff?"

"I think Xander's open to giving us a few pointers. As to how far I'll be willing to go, I don't know."

"You can't tell me that you didn't like what you saw last night."

Logan glanced over at her and laughed, that sexy, rough tone making her heartbeat speed up. "Baby, I buried my cock in your pussy; I don't think there was any disguising the fact that I liked it. I won't deny that. That doesn't mean you'd enjoy it if you were in Mercedes's shoes."

"Are they together?" Sam asked.

"I don't know."

"If they aren't, do you think you would reconsider Xander for a threesome?"

*"No. Sam, Xander's not the right man for what you're thinking. He's a Dom. He's not going to willingly walk into a situation where he isn't in control. And you know I'm not willing to give up control."*

After that conversation, they had been back twice. Once on Wednesday for what had been dubbed Devotion's BDSM theme night and again last night.

On Wednesday, their attendance had been more of a social gathering. Not that there was anything wrong with socializing, because, other than work, there wasn't much else that she did besides hang out with her best friend, Sierra, and Sierra's husbands, Luke and Cole, or sit around and chat with Ashleigh and Alex, Tag and McKenna, and even Kane and Lucie from time to time.

So, yes, her life revolved around spending time with her friends. Or going to the club. Or both. Just not this often.

Then there was last night's adventure, which had been preplanned, and Sam had enjoyed herself, even if the night — or more accurately, Logan's mood — had taken a strange turn. Again, she got the impression it was from the man who'd come into their room and watched them.

Ever since that conversation with Logan, Sam had been trying to figure out what was going on. Logan was waffling on what he wanted, or so it seemed to her. Based on what she gathered from talking to Logan, they needed a little time to figure out what it was they both wanted. Away from the allure of the club.

Logan apparently wasn't on the same page.

Although Sam had been surprised by Logan's renewed interest in going to Devotion last night, she'd found his suggestion a little coincidental since it had followed right on the heels of his most recent visit to X-hale, Xander Boone's infamous cigar bar, where the boys liked to hang out.

From the moment Logan had stepped foot in the house Thursday night, Sam had realized he was simmering with anticipation. She'd tried to pry out of him the reason for his sudden eagerness, but he wouldn't tell her.

But Sam could put two and two together. It wasn't all that difficult.

Coincidentally, last night Logan had been talking to the attractive dark-haired man, who, also coincidentally, had played voyeur to their private party. She knew somehow that man played a part in all of this; it just didn't explain why she hadn't received a formal introduction to him.

So, of course, as soon as Logan had told her that he wanted to take her to Devotion tonight, Sam had called Sierra.

*"We're going to the club tonight. Will you be there?"*

*"Yes. Luke and Cole want to be there for a few days since the club just opened. My mom's watching Hannah so I can join them. Why? Are you going?"*

*"Yes," Sam confirmed.*

*"Awesome. I guess I'll see you in a little while."*

*"Wait, Sierra. I've got a question."*

*"I might just have an answer," Sierra said with a laugh.*

*"There was a man there last night. Attractive. Dark hair, scruffy face, light brown eyes. He was wearing a dark suit but no tie. Do you know who he is?"*

*"Not off the top of my head, no," Sierra told her. "I met a lot of new people last night, though. Why?"*

*"No reason," Sam lied.*

*"Uh-huh." Sierra chuckled. "All right. I'll see you in a bit then."*

After that call was complete, Sam had headed for the shower. Now, an hour later, clad in her black silk robe, Sam had just finished meticulously applying her makeup while Logan showered.

All the while, her mind had been spinning with a myriad of questions.

*Who was the sexy stranger?*

*Why was Logan suddenly hell-bent on going to Devotion?*

*Did it really have something to do with him?*

Turning around to face the shower, Sam leaned against the bathroom counter and folded her arms beneath her breasts while she studied Logan momentarily. From her vantage point, she could admire her husband's incredibly sexy, nude body while he showered. And she could also ask him questions, which was what she decided to do.

"Remember the conversation we had last week on the way to work? After opening night at Devotion? The one where you told me to think long and hard?" she asked, raising her voice to be heard over the water.

"I remember," he said, his voice echoing against the tiled walls while he lathered shampoo into his dark hair.

"I wanted to talk about our options. You know, the whole *it's either BDSM or a threesome* thing."

"I never meant you had to choose between them, Sam," Logan answered with a heavy sigh, his eyes now meeting hers across the steamy bathroom. "I was referring to a threesome with Xander *or* BDSM. I wasn't drawing a line between BDSM and a threesome. And I *never* said it had to be one or the other."

The shower water turned off, and Sam watched as Logan grabbed one of the oversized bath towels that she'd bought on sale just last week. He raked the slate-gray cotton through his hair and then ran it over his firm, lean body, catching Sam's attention with his every move.

"I know," she told him, not even attempting to disguise the fact that she was ogling him.

And she really did know what he was saying. Logan hadn't given her an ultimatum by any means, but she had been under the impression that he was trying to sway her one way or the other. "Are you really interested in BDSM?" she asked.

"Did you not enjoy last night?" Logan's dark eyebrows shot up; a look of unrestrained carnality glowed on his face. It was a look that she knew very, very well.

He was clearly remembering that swing.

"I did enjoy it. Very much," she explained, feeling her face heat from embarrassment. Yes, she was quite fond of trying new things, but it didn't make talking about them any easier.

After her up-close-and-personal introduction to BDSM, Sam had certainly been looking forward to learning more. And that was the main reason they'd gone back on Wednesday. For theme night. Just to watch.

Granted, last night had been better. More intense. She had been tied up in a swing, so it could probably be classified as bondage. But something else — that man coming in to watch — had been what tipped the scales for her. That had made it incredible.

Sam wasn't ashamed to admit that her inner nympho was quite fond of the lifestyle Logan had introduced her to.

"So you liked when I tied you up and had my wicked way with you?" he asked with a curiously wicked gleam in his eyes.

"I always like when you have your wicked way with me. Tied up or not." Sam grinned. Logan was tenacious when he wanted something, and he made her burn for him with just a look. "But that's the thing... I don't have to be tied up."

There was no denying how hot the scene with Mercedes and Xander had been, nor would she pretend that she hadn't been incredibly turned on by it. It just wasn't quite what she'd thought it would be. It seemed to work for Xander and Mercedes, but Sam hadn't been able to imagine her and Logan doing the same thing.

Logan frowned. "Do you not want me to tie you up?"

"That's not what I'm saying," Sam said, her frustration coming through in her clipped tone. "I just..." She couldn't find the words to finish that sentence.

Yes, she was definitely screwing this all up.

# CHAPTER THREE

Up until Logan had point-blank told her that Xander would not be a candidate for a third in their relationship, Sam had been anticipating the possibility of another threesome. And then that man had come in last night, his mere presence heightening Sam's pleasure tenfold. The way he watched her and the way Logan watched her... The presence of that man hadn't just affected her, it had affected Logan, too.

That's when it had all come back full circle for her. Back to the day she'd met Logan and the subsequent days that had followed.

There were so many things that Logan did to her that made her crave him, both then and now, but truthfully, the look in his beautiful eyes had always been what made Sam burn hotter. She could get lost in Logan's penetrating gaze for hours. It was a heady feeling when he turned his full attention on her, all but consuming her with a heated look.

"It just seems like we're trying too hard." God, she was doing a horrible job of explaining this. "Last night was mind-blowing. Better than anything we've done in a long time. But it didn't have anything to do with being tied up."

Sam allowed a small amount of disappointment to show when Logan wrapped his towel around his waist. He laughed at her, just as she'd hoped he would.

"What did it have to do with then?"

They stared at one another for a long moment before Sam finally said, "That man. It had to do with that man."

Logan nodded, his eyes still fixed on her as he added, "You're still interested in a threesome."

It wasn't a question, just a simple statement, and to her surprise, Logan didn't sound disappointed. Not that she'd really expected him to. They could create a spark between them alone just as well as when they were around others. That had never been an issue. But they both knew that what had transpired between them back when Luke and then Tag had been in their lives had been volatile.

"Yes," she told him just to assure him that they were thinking the same thing. "I'm still interested in a threesome."

Logan's head tilted slightly, his eyes locked with hers. "Finish getting ready and we'll talk some more."

Sam wondered if he had something specific that he wanted to talk about or if he was just interested in digging deeper into her psyche. He did that. Logan liked to know everything she was thinking. If he had a concern, he confronted her about it.

Logan didn't like her hiding from him, and he made a point to remind her that she couldn't keep herself from him. So, for the last couple of years, she'd grown accustomed to opening up to him. Especially when he questioned her openly.

Sam watched him disappear from the bathroom. She did need to finish getting ready or there wouldn't be anyone left at the club for them to go see anyway.

Heading to her closet to get dressed, she thought back to the last part of their conversation last week.

"I need you to do something for me, Sam," Logan said. "You need to think long and hard about what you want. If you want to pursue this BDSM stuff, I'm game. If you'd prefer to find a third for the future, I'm open to that, too. I just need to know which you want more.

"Unfortunately, I think you're going to have to make a choice here. I don't see you getting both. And definitely not with Xander."

Sam had agreed with him wholeheartedly. It was part of the reason she hadn't pushed further at the time. She did need to give their situation some thought. And she'd done that. She'd actually done little else besides think about it.

Thoughts about what she'd seen that first night, thoughts about what she wanted, what she didn't want, what she might want. It was all very confusing.

Rather than worry about Xander, or whether there might be a possibility for a threesome with him in her future — because she knew without a doubt that the man was in love with Mercedes — she had turned her focus to Logan. Her husband.

It all boiled down to the fact that whatever they decided to do would need to make them both happy.

If BDSM was something they could give a trial run, then maybe they should. But if Logan was doing this to placate her, or because someone else believed it might be what she wanted, they would need to sort that out ahead of time.

Sam wanted what Logan wanted. Pure and simple.

That was when the most important questions had come to her: Was she putting her desires before Logan's? Was Logan doing the same with her? Had they somehow lost sight of what would make them both happy?

Since the very first time when Logan had introduced her to a threesome, she'd found out things about herself that she hadn't even known existed. And she craved those interactions as much as Logan did. Only they'd both shut down somewhere along the way because things hadn't worked out the way she had expected.

That didn't mean Sam wasn't happy. She was. More so than she ever had been in her life. And with each passing day, Logan continued to teach her more and more about herself. Like just how much love she could have for one single human being.

There was no denying the fact that she enjoyed the exhilarating feeling of two men focused on her, the way Logan controlled her pleasure, even if he was just directing her.

She knew Logan enjoyed those times, as well.

But she also knew Logan didn't develop emotional ties the way that she did. At least not with the two men who had previously participated in their sexual exploits. For him, it was about pleasure, and she respected that. Just as he respected the fact that the casual interactions weren't her thing.

They had quickly learned that the whole threesome thing was a double-edged sword. Despite how much they enjoyed it, Sam feared she was going to get hurt.

That was why they had opted to forgo threesomes shortly after Tag had ended their sexcapades. Although she couldn't lie and say that she hadn't thought about them, because she had. A lot. For the last year and a half, she had held out hope that they might get back to that place one day.

She'd actually believed for a short period that they might've reached that point when they were introduced to Xander Boone, an extremely handsome single man whom Sam had found herself attracted to.

At that point, the thoughts of threesomes had returned with a vengeance.

It didn't help that there were many times when she and Logan were alone that he would tell her exactly what he wanted another man to do to her. His deep, rich baritone mixed with his graphic narration always set her aflame. No matter the time or place.

Of course, when she'd found out that Logan had considered propositioning Xander, she'd found the idea intriguing, even if she'd been momentarily terrified. She wasn't scared of Xander, but the thought of what *she* would ultimately want from another untraditional relationship weighed heavily on her mind. After all, they had believed that Xander was an unattached man, and that meant he could move on at any time, especially if love came knocking on his door.

After watching Xander and Mercedes, despite what the two of them had said about their relationship — or more accurately, their *friend*ship — Sam wasn't at all convinced that things between them were strictly platonic.

But that wasn't even the point. It was no longer about Xander. She wasn't interested, and she knew he wasn't, either.

The point was that Sam felt as though she was getting in over her head. Perhaps she was.

It wasn't a secret that their previous threesomes hadn't worked, so she had no clue why she would think it could happen now. Especially because Sam knew deep down that she wanted more from a polyamorous relationship than just sex. Not that she had mentioned that to Logan. Yet.

But then he'd come up with the proposal of BDSM.

She didn't mind experimenting, but was that something they would use to replace the threesomes? Could it be enough to sate those specific urges that the two of them had?

Doubtful.

Double-checking that her mascara hadn't clumped, Sam attempted to rein in her thoughts. Now that she was dressed and ready, she was more than a little excited. Logan had something planned for tonight; she could feel it.

"Are you almost ready?" Logan called from the bedroom, successfully distracting her.

Sam took a step back, staring at the woman in the mirror, her smile not forced. Yep, she was ready. A little too ready. "One minute," she replied, grabbing her brush and running it through her hair one last time. Once she was finished, she stepped into the bedroom to find Logan sitting on the edge of the bed.

"Come here." He beckoned her toward him by crooking his finger and she complied.

With him sitting on the bed and her standing, Sam came to a stop directly in front of him.

"Did you need something?" she asked coyly.

"I want to see what you're wearing," he explained, his hands sliding down over her hips. His hazel eyes had caught fire; the passion and heat she was so familiar with seemed to glow from within.

"Just a dress." One of her favorites, but he already knew that. The short, sequined sheath accentuated her curvy body better than any other dress she owned. If she could get away with it, she would wear it all the time.

"Hmmm, but I'm more interested in what's beneath the dress," Logan said with a mischievous grin.

Beneath? Sam returned the grin, enjoying the feel of Logan's warm hands as they slid under the hem of her dress.

While her toes dug into the plush carpet beneath her bare feet, Sam moaned as Logan's slightly rough fingers roamed over the skin of her upper thighs, higher.

"Logan." His name came out on a breathy moan as she waited ever so impatiently for him to continue.

"I think you should go without these tonight," Logan said as he hooked his fingers beneath the thin string of her thong along her hip.

Sam squeezed her thighs together, halting his progress. Go without panties? Tonight? "I'm not sure that's a good idea," she pleaded.

"I am." His response left no room for argument, and her body temperature rose even higher.

She loved the demanding side of Logan, the side that told her how much control he had over her. That didn't mean she wouldn't argue her point a little. It's what she did. "What if I refuse?" she whispered.

"Then I'll rip them right off of you," he advised, his voice low and even, not at all threatening. It was a promise. A small smile tipped the corners of his mouth.

As much as she liked the idea, over the course of their marriage, Logan had ruined more than one pair of her panties, and she really was getting tired of replacing them.

"I'll take them off," she informed him as she tried to take a step back. His hands tightened on her hips, stilling her.

"I think I'd rather do the honors."

Oh, hell. They might not make it out of the house if he kept this up.

Giving in, Sam stood still while Logan took his time lowering her panties until they slipped over her calves and landed on her feet. Stepping out of them, she grabbed them with her toes and lifted her foot, laughing with him while he took them from her. His other hand continued to roam beneath the dress, his fingers tormenting her mound as he brushed gently over her bare skin.

"Are you ready to go?" he asked, a grin splitting his face because clearly he knew exactly what he did to her.

"I am," she assured him. More than ready.

Logan rose to his feet, but when she turned to head for the door, he stopped her by placing his hand on her arm.

"You won't need this tonight, either," he said, his other hand sliding down her back, stopping on the strap of her bra.

Oh, hell.

Sam sucked in a deep breath and nodded. Arguing with him was a losing battle. Logan always got what he wanted. He had a way of making her melt into a puddle, which meant she would eventually cave. She'd learned not to pretend otherwise because it was a waste of time.

Logan slid the narrow straps of her dress down her arms, the silk effortlessly dropping past her breasts. He then easily unclasped her strapless bra and tossed it onto the bed. When his arms came around her, Sam leaned back into his embrace, relishing the feel of his warm hands on her naked breasts.

He was teasing her. On purpose.

Thankfully, he didn't linger long. If he had, Sam wasn't so sure they'd have made it out of the house. In fact, Logan went from relaxed to determined in the blink of an eye. So much so, Sam was surprised he even allowed her to put on her shoes, giving her barely enough time to strap them on before he was ushering her out of the house and into the Corvette.

She slid into the sleek car after he opened her door and let her head drop back on the headrest.

This was going to be one of those nights; she could feel it already.

# CHAPTER FOUR

"ELIJAH PENN, I'D LIKE YOU TO MEET my wife, Samantha."

Elijah noticed the way Sam's eyes widened as her gaze strayed to his face. That was without doubt surprise glowing mysteriously in her eyes. Reaching out, Elijah took Sam's hand, lifting it to his mouth as he kept his gaze locked with hers. He was supposed to say something; he knew that. He just couldn't find the words.

"I invited him here tonight," Logan explained. "The same as last night."

Samantha retrieved her hand from his grasp, and Elijah continued to watch her.

"Very nice to meet you, Samantha," Elijah managed when he found his voice. "Would you mind if I buy you a drink?"

After turning to look at Logan briefly, Samantha leveled her stare on him once more. "I'd like that," she said sweetly, linking her fingers with Logan's tightly.

Elijah's cock wasn't the only part of his anatomy that had stood at attention as soon as he had laid eyes on Samantha McCoy in the shadows of the dimly lit club. His entire body was rock hard.

Thankfully, he had his jacket in place to hide the physical evidence of his arousal. But the jacket was doing little to keep his interest on the down low.

Elijah followed the couple to an empty table.

The three of them had managed to find an empty table in a relatively quiet spot where the music wasn't blaring obnoxiously overhead. It also gave them a little privacy. Not that they needed it.

He waited for Samantha to take her seat before he lowered himself into the chair beside her. Yeah, he was pretty sure that shielding himself wasn't doing much good, because he could tell that the incredibly beautiful woman now seated beside him knew just how much she affected him. Both last night and tonight.

And she had.

More than he'd expected.

A waitress arrived instantly, taking their drink order and scurrying off. The awkward silence had nearly strangled him by the time the woman returned.

"Thank you," Sam told him when the waitress delivered their drinks. "For the drink."

Elijah grinned, glancing away from Sam and down to his drink now sitting in front of him, thankful for the shadows that partially hid his face. He didn't know what Samantha might read in his expression, but he knew it would likely be enough to send her running in the opposite direction.

Elijah had absolutely no idea what it was, but his response to Samantha was... God, it was fucking unexpected. That's what it was.

"My pleasure," he told her, his gaze sliding up to meet hers once again.

Logan had mentioned more than once just how incredibly beautiful his wife was, but Elijah knew men did that all the time. In a husband's eyes, his wife should be the most beautiful woman in the world. From experience, Elijah had expected Samantha to be pretty. He had not, however, expected her to be quite as resplendent as she was.

The woman was magnificent when she was naked — something he had learned last night — but she was even more radiant in that short, shiny dress.

Okay, so maybe Samantha wasn't drop-dead, supermodel gorgeous, but she was incredibly attractive. More so than her outer beauty, there was something in her eyes, something that had reached out and grabbed ahold of him by his shirt collar. He wasn't sure what it was, but he'd be damned if he knew what to do about it.

When he'd arrived at Devotion tonight, he had half expected to find out that he had imagined all of it. The way she had pulled him under her spell with just a look. It had been real. Very real.

"Tell me a little about yourself," Sam said, her eyes darting over to Logan and then back to him. "I'm afraid my husband hasn't told me anything about you."

"That doesn't surprise me," Elijah said softly, smiling back at her. "I just met him last week."

"The two of you *just* met?" Sam asked dubiously, her voice rising an octave or two as she glanced between the two of them.

"Technically, yes," Logan answered ruefully. "However, I've known *of* Elijah for quite some time."

Samantha laughed. "Well, that makes it all better then."

"You could say we're business associates, although we hadn't met face-to-face until the other night," Elijah provided, smiling back at her.

"You're..." Sam's eyes widened as her sentence trailed off.

Elijah raised his eyebrows, encouraging her to continue.

"Elijah Penn." Sam said his name, a hint of recognition in her tone as she looked at Logan, who merely nodded. "Ahh, interesting. You're with Virtual Impact."

*Interesting?*

"I am." Elijah wasn't sure he needed to add any more to that.

Sam's smile confirmed it. "Well, it's nice to put a face with a name. I've known *of you* for quite some time, too."

"I hope what you've heard has been good," he teased.

"That depends," Sam offered teasingly. "If XTX got the deal they were looking for, it was wonderful. If not... Well, you understand."

Elijah laughed. Yes, he understood all too well. It was business. "I guess since you aren't running from the table, it wasn't bad enough to make you send me on my way."

"If it were, I wouldn't be sitting here now."

Elijah believed her. Just the look in her pretty green eyes told him she didn't say things she didn't mean. And if Samantha didn't like him, he already knew she wasn't the type of woman who would sit there and pretend that she did.

"I guess it goes without saying that you're a member of Devotion?" Again, Samantha glanced back and forth between him and Logan.

"I didn't have to jump anyone at the door to get in, no."

Samantha laughed, a hearty sound that sent an odd shiver down Elijah's spine. What was it about this woman?

"Since you're a member, I don't have to assume that you're interested in... What *are* you interested in, Mr. Penn?"

"Call me Eli, please," he replied. Lowering his voice just a hint, he leaned in a little closer. "I'm interested in whatever you're willing to offer."

Samantha's sharp inhale made his body harden. She wasn't offended; that much he could tell.

"Since you obviously enjoy watching," Samantha began, her voice lowered the same way his had been, "I'm wondering whether you like to participate."

"Is that what you're offering?" he asked bluntly.

"If I am?"

"Then I'd say I'd love to participate with you." Elijah glanced up at Logan then, noticing the other man was smiling. He was trying to hide it, but it was there.

Returning his attention to Samantha, he added, "And after watching such a magnificent scene last night, I will admit I'm quite anxious."

Not that Elijah would actually make a move tonight. Tonight was about meeting her, getting to know her a little. Then, if things went well from there, he'd be in touch with Logan tomorrow. Or vice versa.

As far as he was concerned, he was ready to go home with them tonight.

And wasn't that fucking crazy?

---

SAM WAS STILL A LITTLE IN SHOCK. And the reason her equilibrium was slightly askew had more to do with Elijah and the fact that Logan had clearly set up this introduction. Only he'd intended for them to meet last night.

Nice way to be introduced. Naked, while a man watched her husband give her an explosive orgasm.

Wait. "Question. If you're so interested, what happened last night? I can only assume that we were supposed to be officially introduced after you stumbled upon us."

She'd learned a long time ago to always expect the unexpected from Logan. After all, that's how she'd been introduced to Luke and Tag, respectively.

Elijah looked away briefly. When his eyes met hers again, he looked contrite. "I hope you'll forgive me for my behavior last night. I panicked."

"Panicked? Because I was naked?"

Elijah laughed. "Not at all. In fact, I've never seen anything hotter."

Even the memory made her body temperature soar. Taking a sip of her drink, she tried to cool herself somewhat while she waited for him to continue.

"I just got a little lost in my thoughts. That's all."

Sam had no idea what that meant, but she didn't want Elijah to feel as though this were an interrogation, so she opted to let it go. For now.

"I take it the two of you have talked a little more than in passing?" She already knew the answer, and it absolutely explained Logan's anticipation about last night.

"We have," Elijah answered. "Your husband speaks his mind."

"When I find something I want, I tend to go after it," Logan admitted. "And when Sam wants something, I pull out all of the stops."

Sam leaned slightly into Logan, who was standing behind her. "I'm not fooled," Sam told Elijah. "He's very protective of me. Despite his present excitement, I know this wasn't a spur-of-the-moment decision."

"I doubt it was, too," Elijah stated as he glanced behind her to Logan.

Sam couldn't help but notice the slight hint of an accent, one that had little to do with being in America and more to do with somewhere else entirely. "Where are you from?" she found herself asking curtly.

"I was born and raised in the UK," he confirmed.

Yep, undeniably a British accent. Or at least what was left of one. "You've been in the US for a while, huh?"

"Since I was twenty-three."

Sam nodded as she tried to decipher just how old that would make him. Since she had nothing else to reference, the math wasn't going to work out. By the way that Elijah's golden-brown eyes twinkled, she figured he knew what she was aiming for.

She could tell he was older than she was. He was probably older than Logan was, but not by much.

"I'm forty-two."

Yep, he knew. Sam smiled, and she knew she looked incredibly guilty, but Elijah didn't seem to mind at all.

Before she could question him on a more personal level, Trent Ramsey sidled up to the table, beer in hand and a huge smirk on his face.

"Elijah. Sam. Good to see you," he greeted.

When the actor didn't address Logan, Sam glanced over her shoulder and noticed that Logan wasn't behind her as he had been a minute earlier.

"He said he'd be right back," Elijah told her.

Sam watched him, trying to figure out how he would've heard that if she hadn't. She didn't get a chance to ask when Trent addressed Elijah once again.

"If you have a few minutes later this week, I'd like to talk. If not, I'll catch up with you next week."

"I'll be around," Elijah told him. "Unless something changes, I'll be here until Thursday."

Sam wasn't paying much attention to what the two men were talking about. She was too busy admiring her present company.

God, the man was incredibly handsome. And she wasn't talking about the pretty-boy actor, either. Everyone knew Trent Ramsey was a good-looking man, but she was referring to Elijah Penn.

The man was... He was devastatingly attractive; there was no doubt about it. With his short, dark hair, those golden-brown eyes that seemed intently focused on her, his dark eyebrows, and long, black eyelashes, he was well put together. Sam was just as fascinated by the heavy, dark stubble along his jaw and chin and the bronze color of his skin that said he spent quite a bit of time outdoors.

But there was something else about Elijah that caught her breath. Almost as though there was a vulnerability that he wasn't trying all that hard to hide. Sam clearly didn't know him well enough to know whether she was reading him correctly, though. Obviously, Logan must've felt comfortable with the man because he'd left her alone with him, so Sam figured for now, she'd go with it.

"Good to see you again, Samantha."

Sam looked over in time to see Trent waving as he walked away, a devilish glint in his eyes.

Yes, she'd clearly just been caught eyeing Elijah. By Trent, no less.

What that said about her, she didn't even want to think about.

Before she had to do just that, Logan walked up, placing his warm, comforting hand on her back.

"Well, it's getting late. I really didn't want to keep you out tonight, but it was pertinent that I get to meet you. To apologize," Elijah said, his full attention once again on her. "If you'd be so inclined, I'd love to see you again, Samantha."

*So inclined?* Okay, now she was speechless.

Logan's hand slid into her hair, his fingers twining gently through the strands, and Sam realized he was just touching her for the sake of touching her. She turned to look up at him, and the heat she saw in his eyes told her exactly what he was looking forward to.

Turning back to Elijah, Sam said, "I'd like that, too."

And that was the understatement of the century.

---

BEFORE ELIJAH COULD GET AWAY SO QUICKLY, Logan spoke up. "Why don't we stay for a while? We can go check out what's going on."

Sam looked at him inquisitively, but Logan just smiled down at his wife. For whatever reason, Logan wasn't ready to call it a night. Not just yet.

He was very much aware of the attraction between Sam and Elijah. It was plainly written on both of their faces. And after last night, Logan wasn't quite ready for Elijah to disappear again. It seemed to be something he did often, and Logan had a feeling it was due to the man's desire to keep himself isolated. He'd probably been that way ever since his wife had passed away.

"What did you have in mind?" Elijah asked, hiding his surprise well as he came to his feet when Sam did.

"Nothing specific. Rumor has it that Mercedes has reserved one of the glass rooms tonight. I'm curious as to what they're going to do."

Sam looked up at him, studying him. He had no doubt that she had figured out he was stalling. But thankfully, she didn't call him on it.

For the next few minutes, the three of them weaved their way through the crowd, stopping to talk to people they recognized. Logan introduced Elijah to anyone he didn't know, which, as it turned out, was quite a few people.

Logan was heading toward the main attraction — the glass-enclosed rooms — when he heard Mercedes talking to Shane Gibson.

"Care to watch?" she asked Shane as Logan, Sam, and Elijah moved closer.

"Depends. As much as I'd love to see you beat his ass, I'm waiting for someone. She should be here any minute. If you can wait a few minutes, I'd be happy to watch. Or even participate."

*Beat his ass? What the hell was going on?*

"We'd like to watch," Sam said rather loudly, apparently talking to Mercedes.

Okay, so that had been a little unexpected. But what the hell.

"Is that right?" Mercedes spoke to Sam, a beaming smile on her pretty face.

"If that's all right with you, of course," Sam amended.

"I've reserved room three," Mercedes informed Sam, her hand waving toward the glass rooms behind them. "If you'd like, you can have a front-row seat."

"We'll be in a private room upstairs." Logan looked over at Elijah, surprised that the man had spoken up.

"A private room?" Samantha asked, clearly as surprised as Logan was by his revelation.

"That's right," Elijah answered. "That is, if you're game."

Samantha turned to look at Logan, and the only thing he could do was nod in response. He was curious as hell to find out what Elijah had planned.

"There's my date now," Shane said, and Logan turned to see whom he was referring to.

A petite brunette joined them, greeting both Mercedes and Shane.

"Well, we'll likely catch up with you later," Logan offered, ready to make his way to that private room Elijah had referred to.

"We look forward to watching your scene, as well," Mercedes said to Logan, her attention divided between him and Elijah.

Yeah, he doubted the foursome would spend any time worried about what Logan and Sam were about to do. The heat that was generating between them was going to keep them occupied for the foreseeable future.

Taking Sam's hand, Logan began to retreat from the foursome. He looked over to see that Elijah had taken her other hand.

It obviously didn't take much, because that simple gesture had Logan's blood pressure spiking.

The three of them made their way up the stairs, and with every passing step, Logan's cock thickened. This was a first. Usually he was the one in control, making the decisions and planning things in advance.

Apparently, he'd met his match with Elijah.

When they reached the third door on the right, Elijah released Sam's hand and turned to face her. He didn't spare Logan even a single glance, which surprised him.

"I'd like to make up for my disappearance last night by requesting a repeat."

Sam's eyes widened, but she didn't look away from Elijah.

"This room doesn't have a swing, but I'm sure Logan can get creative."

Sam did look up at him then. Logan met her gaze. "Up to you, baby."

Sam looked back at Elijah, and the next thing Logan knew, she was nodding her head.

Elijah took her hand once again and led her into the room. Once they were inside, Elijah closed the door behind them, effectively sealing them off from any prying eyes.

This was definitely private.

Feeling the need to regain some control of the evening, Logan pulled Sam against him, cupping her face as he stared down at her. "Is this what you want?" he asked, not trying to keep his voice low.

"Yes," she murmured, exhilaration echoing in her beautiful eyes.

"Good," he said, hoping he sounded encouraging. At the moment, he just wanted to strip her bare and drive himself into her. It had been a long damn time since they'd done this. Since another man had been involved.

Although tonight, he didn't intend to allow Elijah to be too involved. After all, last night had just been for his viewing pleasure. Until Logan was comfortable with the man's intentions, Elijah wouldn't be putting his hands on Sam.

Elijah knew it, too.

There was a king-sized bed on one wall, a long row of cabinets along another, and a single chair in the room.

"Have a seat." Logan gestured toward the chair, his instruction meant for Elijah. "I want you on the bed, baby. But first, I want you naked."

Sam stared back at him, uncertainty etched into her features.

"Take off your dress," he instructed, which he figured was what she was waiting for.

A small smile tipped the corner of her mouth as she eased the straps down her shoulders until the sequined dress was sliding down her body. He loved those damn dresses. The ones she wore that took very little effort to get off her.

"Fuck," Elijah whispered.

Yeah, that's exactly what Logan thought every time Sam undressed for him. "Now up on the bed. I want you to sit on the edge so that Elijah has a front-row seat."

Sam glanced over at Elijah and then back to Logan. She knew she only had to say no and they wouldn't go any further.

She didn't say no.

Logan bit the inside of his cheek as Sam eased up onto the bed, her legs dangling over the side. "Now lie back."

Sam lay flat on her back.

Logan's hunger for this woman detonated. Seeing her there, seeing Elijah watching. It was what he'd been waiting to do for so long.

Logan made his way between Sam's legs, pushing her knees farther apart with his thighs. When he was content with how exposed she was, he slid his hands beneath her thighs and lifted her legs up before pushing them back toward her, placing her on full display.

"I'm a hungry man, baby." Logan growled the words, his need to taste her making him crazy. Leaning down, still holding her legs back, Logan pressed his mouth to her pussy. He lapped at her, licking her like a lollipop repeatedly before zeroing in on that tiny bundle of nerves now peeking out at him.

"Logan!" Sam cried out, her hands covering his as though she was trying to help him hold her. He didn't need help, but it did prove just how hot she was.

All because Elijah was sitting there watching them.

"So fucking sweet," he groaned as he continued to torment her with his tongue. "God, baby, I could fuck you with my tongue all night."

Sam moaned loudly as her body thrashed against the bed. Logan didn't let up; he teased her clit, lashing at it with his tongue, sucking it between his lips. He had no idea how many minutes passed, but he knew he wasn't done yet.

"Hold your legs back," he commanded Sam, releasing her thighs as he stood to his full height.

"I want you to watch Elijah while I fuck you with my fingers, Sam. Watch how hot he gets from seeing my fingers slide deep inside of your wet pussy."

Logan teased her entrance briefly before slipping two fingers inside of her, the walls of her pussy clamping down on him, pulling him deeper. When her eyes met Elijah's, Logan began to fuck her. A slow, steady pace, his fingers going in deep while he used his other thumb to rub her engorged clit.

"Logan," Sam cried, never taking her eyes off Elijah, and that damn near made Logan come right in his fucking pants.

"Are you ready to come for me?"

"Yes. Oh, God, yes. Please make me come."

That's exactly what Logan did. He made his wife come undone while another man watched.

# CHAPTER FIVE

"HEY, LADY," SAM GREETED SIERRA THE FOLLOWING Saturday morning when her sister-in-law walked through her front door. "Come here, beautiful girl," she cooed to Hannah as she reached out to take the baby from Sierra's arms.

It was hard to believe that Hannah was already three months old, and in that short amount of time, she'd grown into a very expressive, beautiful bundle of perfection.

Taking her from Sierra, Sam cuddled her close and smothered her with kisses as she headed back toward the kitchen, where she'd been working on her laptop.

"How are things?" Sam asked Sierra as she took a seat across from her, dropping the bulky diaper bag onto the table.

"Never better," Sierra said with an award-winning smile.

Sam was brimming with excitement, anxious to tell Sierra all about Elijah and what had happened on Monday, but she was still nervous about saying it aloud for fear that she might jinx herself. She had actually had a phone conversation with Elijah just two days ago, and since then, she'd been hovering on the brink of exploding with the urge to tell her best friend.

God, Sam couldn't stop thinking about him.

Logan had made sure she didn't stop thinking about him, too. When they'd arrived home from the club on Monday night, he'd seduced her with his sexy words, graphically describing all of the things he and Elijah would be doing to her in the very near future.

"I heard you had yourself a date the other night," Sierra stated, pulling Sam right out of her daydream.

"Logan and I tend to have date nights quite frequently," Sam replied, knowing full well that Sierra was alluding to something besides her many date nights with her husband.

"Hot ones, at that. I heard you have a penchant for the swing," Sierra teased.

Sam laughed, trying to hide her embarrassment. Despite the fact that she'd come into her own and enjoyed herself openly, there were still moments like this that made her very aware of how much of herself she'd shown lately.

Rather than respond, Sam decided to redirect as she glanced down at the baby and laughed. "I heard *you* requested your husbands to buy you a Sybian saddle machine."

"Oh, don't even get me started on that," Sierra beamed. "You have got to try it."

"Until Logan told me about it, I had no idea what it even was. But you... Oh, my God, did you...?" Sam hadn't stuck around long the other night, but she had heard from Logan that Sierra was quite fond of the new toy that her husbands had introduced her to.

Sierra laughed. "No. Well, yes, but no."

"What does that mean?" Sam asked, amused by the way Sierra stumbled over her words.

"I did try it. *After* the club was closed."

"And?"

"And what? It was freaking amazing. Like I said, you have to try it."

"Maybe next time," Sam said, knowing there wasn't a chance in hell of that happening. "But if I were you, I wouldn't let Trent hear you go on and on about how great it was," Sam joked.

Trent Ramsey, one of the investors in the Devotion club, had been the one who'd requested the strange piece of machinery be included in the BDSM theme night. He'd bragged that women would flock to it. According to what she'd heard, Trent had been right, but they all preferred not to let him know when he was right. He would never let them forget it.

"Don't worry, I won't."

Sam smiled down at Hannah. The beautiful little girl looked so tiny resting comfortably in her arms. "My goodness, she's gotten so big."

"Tell me about it," Sierra laughed. "If she gets much bigger, I'm not going to be able to tote her around."

"You're almost as big as your mommy, you know that?" Sam whispered to the sleepy baby as she pressed another kiss to Hannah's smooth chubby cheek. Looking back up at Sierra, Sam asked, "How are the boys?"

"Good. This week's been a little hectic for them. They aren't used to being at the club every night."

"How long are they planning to keep that up?"

"Probably not much longer. Last night, when they got home to find Hannah asleep, they were disappointed. Her schedule isn't meshing well with theirs."

"I can imagine. Are they hiring someone to handle things for them?"

"They're looking. I don't think either of them is in a hurry. It's not easy to find someone like Kane, you know. Someone they can trust to manage it while they aren't there. This is their livelihood."

"Well, they can always take turns," Sam teased. "Then again, I have noticed how ... open the three of you have been lately. I guess all that time working together makes the sparks fly, huh?"

Sam smiled when Sierra blushed crimson.

Sam immediately remembered the sight of Cole on his knees in front of Luke... A flash of heat spiked in her bloodstream. And then on Monday night, Sam had gotten a glimpse of her sister-in-law, and it was difficult to miss the fact that Sierra had been having a good time, too.

"I'm surprised you noticed," Sierra said as she got up and went to the refrigerator. "You seemed a little ... preoccupied."

Okay, so she'd been busted. It wasn't as if Sam hid anything from Sierra anyway. Not only were they sisters-in-law, but they had become nearly inseparable ever since Sierra had come into their lives.

"Ummm ... Sam?"

Sam looked up to face Sierra, lifting her eyebrow in question.

"You're blushing," she whispered conspiratorially with a huge grin.

"Oh, hush," Sam laughed, turning her attention back to Hannah. "I am not."

"You so are." Sierra sat back down with a bottle of water. "I didn't realize you knew Elijah Penn."

Sierra didn't phrase it as a question, but Sam felt the urge to explain. "I was introduced to him on Monday. He's the guy I was asking you about. Apparently Logan met him when the boys went to X-hale." Sam was not going to go into details about how Elijah had watched while Logan had made her scream his name.

"And?"

"And what?"

"What do you think about him? The three of you seemed a little cozy."

Glancing over at Sierra, Sam decided to spill. "I definitely hope to get to know him better," she said with a guilty smile. It wasn't like Sierra didn't already know that Sam and Logan had been hoping to find a third who would work for them.

"Do you think Elijah might be the one?" Sierra asked, looking both curious and concerned.

"I'm not sure anyone will be 'the one,'" Sam answered softly. "But I think he's interested. As are we."

In all the time she'd been with Logan, Sam had learned a lot about herself. A hell of *a lot.* Some things she'd learned even surprised her. Like the fact that she really, really enjoyed the threesome interactions. And she craved having two men focused on her, with Logan there to ground her. Those moments were unlike anything she'd ever expected.

"I'm interested in getting to know him better. Seeing where it might lead," Sam finally told Sierra.

"Do you think this could be the start of a more permanent friendship?" Sierra asked, a hint of empathy in her tone.

Sam knew Sierra had a good reason to ask that question. Along with finding out about her own kinky side, Sam had also learned that she didn't like the fact that Luke and Tag had both just waltzed right through her life.

Sam loved Logan with every ounce of herself, but she'd made a connection with Luke and then with Tag. It wasn't the same as what she felt for Logan, but she didn't like the idea of getting attached to anyone only so they could move on. And by attached, Sam meant that she'd developed feelings for them. Not love, but she feared that was only because of how brief their encounters were.

And maybe that's why the idea of Elijah scared her a little. Despite the fact that she had really enjoyed his company the other night, not to mention the little show they'd put on for him, she was still wary.

"There're no guarantees, I know, but I don't see how it could hurt to see how things go," Sam told her.

"Well, I won't argue with you there. So, does that mean you're going to pursue this further?"

The only thing Sam knew for fact was that she was open to new experiences, and there was something about Elijah… Did it mean she would be with him? No. It didn't. But it also meant she wasn't going to deny herself the opportunity of getting to know him better since she and Logan both considered him worth pursuing.

Sam wasn't sure what was going to happen. They'd left the club agreeing to see Elijah again but not setting a firm date. And after their scorching-hot moment at home, Sam was inclined to believe that Logan was right with her in thinking ... the sooner the better.

As though he were summoned by her thoughts, the back door that led to the garage opened and Logan walked in, a huge grin on his face as soon as he laid eyes on Hannah. Since the moment Hannah had made her arrival in the world, Logan had been completely smitten with her.

"Wow, this is a wonderful surprise," he said as he walked over to Sam, leaning in and kissing her on the lips, then carefully taking Hannah from her arms. He nuzzled the baby — who looked so tiny in Logan's big arms — close to his chest, his giant hand cupping the back of her head.

"Hey, Sierra," Logan greeted, sparing Sierra a quick glance before devoting himself fully to the little chubby baby in his arms.

"Hi."

"I've got a surprise for you, little one," Logan said as he walked out of the kitchen with Hannah in his arms.

"He bought her some toys the other day when we were out. Yes, he knows she's too little to appreciate them fully, but he insisted."

Sierra's eyes turned soft and Sam knew what was coming.

"Have you two given any more thought to having kids? I mean, I know you've said you didn't want to, but you're both so good with Hannah."

Sam smiled. "And just like every other time you've asked that," Sam chuckled, "no, we don't plan to have kids."

It wasn't that they had anything against children, because, yes, just like Logan, Sam loved every second she got to spend with her niece, but she truly didn't want to have any children of her own. With her career in full swing, and Logan's, too, they knew it wasn't what was best for a child. They were too selfish, and they would be the first to admit it.

"Got it." Sierra laughed, obviously realizing Sam wasn't going to change her mind on the subject. They'd had the same discussion before, and Sam was pretty sure Sierra hoped she would eventually cross over to the mommy side. She and Logan were still content with where they stood on the subject.

Sam went to the fridge and grabbed a bottle of water before returning to the table with Sierra.

"So, tell me something..." Sierra began, glancing back behind her as though Logan might be standing there. When she turned back to face Sam, she continued, "I heard you were part of a scene with Xander and Mercedes."

Sam wasn't quite sure what the question was, so she waited.

"What was it like? Based on what I've seen of them, they're pretty hard-core."

Sam wasn't sure what the definition of hard-core was. She knew that Xander had doled out punishment for whatever reason, and Mercedes had seemed to enjoy herself. But aside from that, she hadn't delved into the reason behind what they'd done.

"You've seen what I've seen," Sam told Sierra. "When we were in the same room together on opening night, it wasn't quite as intense as when Xander strapped her to the spanking bench, but the outcome was still the same. Other than that, I really don't know what to tell you."

"Okay, so clearly you've moved on from the whole BDSM thing."

Had she? Considering the way she'd felt when Elijah had walked into their playroom, yeah, it did seem like she had once again shifted her priorities elsewhere.

"I'm all for experimenting a little," Sam said, blushing as she thought back to the swing. "But, truthfully, I'm not sure it's my thing."

"But Elijah *is* your thing?"

Sam couldn't answer that. She didn't know how to answer that. At least not yet.

"What's he like?"

"Who?"

"Oh, come on. Don't do that. You know who I'm talking about. Elijah."

"I don't know him all that well."

"Yet," Sierra supplied as though reading Sam's mind.

"Yet."

Sierra laughed. "I've never known you to be at a loss for words."

Okay, true.

Sam smiled.

"There's something about him," she admitted, unsure what she really wanted to say.

"Well, I think I figured that out on my own," Sierra replied, leaning back in her chair and pinning Sam with that crystal blue stare.

Sam glanced down at her water bottle and then back up at Sierra. "We didn't talk long, but I'm hopeful that we'll get to talk more," she said quietly.

"Amongst other things?"

Sam laughed. Sierra's mind was in the gutter more often than Sam's was. And that was saying something.

Sierra's features softened as she leaned forward. "Okay, fine. But you're back to thinking about a third? And he's your top candidate?"

He was her *only* candidate. She didn't say that, though.

"I hadn't given it too much thought," she lied. In fact, she had been thinking about Elijah more than she thought was appropriate.

Sam knew her desires were a little out of the norm, at least by most standards, but that didn't stop her from wanting to experience new things. Not that a threesome was new. Not to her or to Logan. And obviously, Logan must've thought Elijah was worth pursuing since he'd introduced them. But she still hadn't had a chance to talk to Logan more. Which she wanted to do before they proceeded.

For over a year, she and Logan hadn't invited anyone else into their relationship, and until recently, she hadn't met anyone that she wanted to interact with that way. As far as she was concerned, Elijah seemed to be interested. And he seemed interested in something more than temporary, but not quite permanent.

Or maybe that was just her wishful thinking.

As for what that meant exactly, she still wasn't sure. But if things worked out the way she hoped, she wouldn't have to worry about a fleeting interlude with someone else.

"What does Logan think of the whole thing?" Sierra asked, interrupting Sam's thoughts.

"What does Logan think of *what* whole thing?" Logan asked as he came into the kitchen holding Hannah and an armful of toys.

Sam glanced at Sierra in time to see her friend blush bright red. Sam laughed and saved her by answering Logan's question. "We were just talking about Elijah."

Logan nodded, lowering himself into a chair beside Sam, his gaze never leaving hers. Sam could see the heat in his eyes and the promise for a little payback for talking about their extracurricular activities later. Sam knew Logan didn't really mind that she talked to Sierra, but that didn't mean he didn't enjoy punishing her, so to speak.

"Speaking of Elijah," Logan said, "we're going to have dinner with him tomorrow night. Then we're going to Devotion."

A sharp flutter erupted in Sam's belly, and she fought the urge to jump out of her chair. Did that mean...?

She didn't want to jump to conclusions. They had gone to Devotion a few times since the club had opened, so that didn't mean they'd be going *with* Elijah after they had dinner with him. She didn't ask, either.

Glancing back at him, she noticed the twinkle in his hazel eyes, and another heatwave flashed through her.

A girl could certainly hope.

LOGAN WATCHED HIS WIFE, AND HE APPRECIATED the effort she made to hide her excitement. The thing was, he knew Sam better than that, and the way her face lit up told him everything he needed to know.

He'd received a phone call from Elijah an hour ago, inviting them to dinner tomorrow, and he had graciously accepted without consulting with Sam first. He knew what her answer would be, and the way her face flushed with heat as she sat across from him confirmed it.

Turning his attention back to Hannah, Logan pretended not to notice. "Where're your daddies, little one?"

"They had to run over to Club Destiny early this morning," Sierra explained. "Kane called and wanted to talk about something."

Logan glanced up at Sierra. "Everything all right?"

"According to Luke, yes." Sierra grinned. "According to Cole, maybe. They both said it really wasn't a big deal. Just a minor incident last night, I guess. Kane handled it, but he wanted to talk with Luke and Cole about it."

Logan nodded. He knew that Kane was quite capable of handling the club now that it had been turned into more of a nightclub than a fetish club. In fact, Kane and Lucie had made some major improvements, from what he'd heard, and Luke seemed quite happy with the two of them managing the place.

"So how are things going with Devotion? Besides the obvious?" he asked, never taking his eyes off Hannah. She was such a beautiful little girl, and she looked so much like Cole it was almost scary. Not that it was a bad thing, but Logan was still surprised sometimes.

"I'm not sure they could be going any better than they are now," Sierra answered before taking a sip of water.

"How's the new house?"

"Lovely. I was telling Sam the other day that there's one down the street that's about to come on the market. I'm thinking we should all be neighbors," Sierra said with a smirk.

"I'm not sure that the neighborhood could handle Luke and me at the same time," Logan joked before glancing back at Hannah. "All right, little one. I've got a meeting. With a golf course. And if I'm late, Alex and your daddies might have my head." He refrained from using the curse words that would've normally spilled from his mouth because of present company.

"How is he doing? Alex?" Sierra asked, her bright blue gaze fixed on him.

Logan knew exactly what she was referring to, but he was pretty sure he didn't have any more information than she did. Less probably. "Today, he seems to be doing fine."

"How is Ashleigh?" Sam asked, directing her question at Sierra.

"I haven't talked to her in a few days. I don't think she's purposely avoiding me, but she's trying to take it easy."

Logan knew that Ashleigh was having a difficult pregnancy, but he'd thought the worst was behind them. Apparently, Alex was either lying or aiming for optimistic. He prayed it was the latter.

"The three of us need to get together for lunch," Sam told Sierra.

"Now, that's what this world needs more of. The three of you together." Logan chuckled as he rose from his seat.

Walking around the table, he handed Hannah back to her mother. "Walk me out?" he asked Sam when his hands were free.

"Of course." She smiled up at him, and he held out his hand to help her up.

When they were in the garage a minute later, Logan backed Sam up against his truck and pressed his body to hers. "If you know what's good for you, you'll be naked when I get home."

"Oh, is that right?" Sam asked with a huge grin on her face.

Pressing his mouth to her ear, Logan mumbled softly, "And if you're a really good girl, you'll be naked *in the hot tub*."

He felt Sam shiver as he nipped her earlobe. God, he loved how responsive she was. Still. Even after all this time, she still responded to him just as she had when they'd first met.

"I might be able to do that," she whispered against his ear. "And then you can tell me all the wicked things you want to do to me."

Logan rumbled, bending his legs and pressing his cock between her thighs, effectively rendering himself useless for the rest of the day. He'd never be able to get his mind off Sam after this, and he already knew his golf game was for shit. "You do know the only reason I'm not fucking you right now is because our niece is in the house, don't you?"

Sam glanced up at him with a grin on her face. "Scared?"

Logan laughed. This woman was going to be the death of him. Planting a quick kiss on her lips, he forced himself to pull back. "Be naked when I get home."

# CHAPTER SIX

"IT'S A DAMN GOOD THING YOU AREN'T a professional golfer," Luke ribbed Logan as they hopped into the golf cart and headed off toward the hole on the ninth green.

"I haven't heard anyone calling to sponsor you, either," Logan nagged his twin. It's what they did, especially when they were on the golf course.

In the cart behind them, Cole and Alex were taking their own sweet time, giving Luke and Logan shit whenever the opportunity arose, which was often.

"I don't answer the phone when they call," Luke declared facetiously.

"Right."

Luke laughed as he pulled the golf cart to a halt. As they climbed out, they both grabbed for a club, but before Logan could move away, Luke turned his attention on him.

"Rumor has it you and Sam are having dinner with Elijah Penn."

Damn, news traveled fast. Then again, Sierra had been at his house when he'd left that morning, so it wasn't all that surprising.

"Yeah," Logan told him. "Problem with that?"

"No," Luke said bluntly. "The question is, do *you* have a problem with that?"

"If I did, do you think we'd be having dinner?"

"Touché."

Logan knew Luke was just looking out for him. Ever since his brother had found his happily ever after, he'd lightened up considerably. It wasn't that Luke was trying to interfere, Logan knew.

"He's got a lot of baggage," Luke said as he stopped on the green.

"I know that," Logan answered. Yes, Elijah had some baggage, and Logan knew that what he might want from Sam would be more than what Luke or Tag had ever wanted, but Logan knew that he was going to have to go on blind faith here. Something told him that this was the right thing to do. Why, he had no fucking clue.

"He still wears his wedding band," Luke stated as he took a few steps forward and lined up with his ball.

Yes, Logan had noticed that. He'd also noticed that when Elijah had been with Sam, he hadn't purposely hidden it from her, but he hadn't made a point to show her, either.

Logan wasn't sure that Luke was expecting a response, so he didn't say anything. Waiting for his brother to putt, Logan glanced back behind him to see Cole and Alex making their way over.

They were laughing, but as they walked up, the two of them sobered quickly. Logan hoped like hell that it wasn't because they were thinking the same thing Luke was.

Logan had given some serious thought to Elijah and what the man would potentially want from Sam — and from him — if they were to pursue this. Despite the nagging voice telling him that this wasn't going to be temporary and it wasn't going to be casual, Logan felt the compelling need to see where it went.

Again, why, he had no idea. It just felt right.

And yes, Logan had already given in to accepting that this would be a relationship. It was what Sam needed. And in turn, what Logan needed also.

"Are you and Sam having problems?" Luke asked pointedly, stunning Logan with his question. He glanced over to see Alex and Cole scrutinizing him carefully.

"No, we're not having problems," Logan barked. "Why the fuck would you ask that?"

"Because you're about to take on a third, who isn't going to be a part-time lover for Sam." Luke's straightforward answer caught Logan off guard.

"Have you talked to Elijah or something?" Logan retorted. "Is there something I don't know here?"

"Man, you were there when he told his story. The guy hasn't moved on after his wife died," Alex offered.

"Would you?" Logan asked candidly. He knew for a fact that if something were to happen to Sam, he wouldn't be a candidate for anything with anyone. Ever again. His wife was his entire world. That wasn't going to change.

Alex glanced down at the ground, "No, I don't think I could, either."

Well, there you had it.

Logan leveled Luke with a stare.

"Are you willing to share her? Completely?" Cole asked, pulling Logan's attention over.

"I am," Logan said flatly. He knew they were looking out for him, and it shouldn't surprise him that the three of them were worried about his decision. Logan had never been interested in something that might turn permanent. And he couldn't necessarily explain why he was now.

"Not just her body," Cole clarified.

"Do you have a hard time sharing Sierra?" Logan bit out.

"No," Cole answered easily. "I don't have a problem sharing Luke with Sierra, either. I love them both. They both love me."

Logan knew where Cole was going with this. When it came down to it, Sam would be in the middle — Logan and Elijah would be sharing her. All of her. For Luke, Cole, and Sierra, it truly was a triangle. One that went all directions.

"Man, you know it's not my place to interfere," Luke bit off. "I just hope you know what you're doing."

"Did you know what you were doing when you hooked up with Sierra and him?" Logan asked, jerking his head in Cole's direction.

Cole laughed and Luke smiled sheepishly as he said, "Point taken."

"It feels right," Logan finally said, walking off toward his ball. It wasn't on the green like the rest of them, so it gave him a minute or two to take a breather.

As Logan ventured away from the trio, he fully expected to panic. Especially after Cole's revelation. But strangely, he didn't.

In terms of being happy, Logan knew that there was something uniquely different about this scenario with Elijah and Sam.

He just couldn't pinpoint exactly what it was.

Yet.

---

WHEN LOGAN ARRIVED home at six o'clock, Sam had ensured that two things were done. One, she had dinner prepared and on the table, and two, she was naked.

Completely.

Just like he'd requested.

She wasn't sure whether he'd really expected her to be, but the flash of desire she saw in his eyes told her that he emphatically approved.

"Fuck. Me," he groaned as he gawked at her from across the room.

"That'll come *after* dinner," she told him deadpan, trying to keep from fidgeting.

Sam wasn't all that keen on being naked, especially when she was doing something as domestic as making dinner, but since she'd met Logan, she'd become more comfortable with it.

Especially when he looked at her like that.

Turning, she led him to the table, feeling the way his eyes raked over every inch of her naked skin.

Taking a deep breath, she took her seat and watched as he joined her after detouring to the kitchen and washing his hands.

"I'm not sure I can stay focused long enough to have dinner," he said, his voice gruff, as he took a seat directly across from her.

"It's your favorite," she told him, amused that he hadn't even noticed. Although Logan was a steak-and-potato kind of guy, she'd learned early on in their marriage that he happened to like her lasagna. She wasn't much of a cook, but she did make a mean lasagna.

When he didn't look down at his plate, she chuckled.

"I remember a certain dinner at this very table that ended in a rather exciting punishment," Logan said, obviously attempting to sound casual.

Sam remembered that dinner well. It was much like this one. The resulting spanking that had followed had been a little unexpected, but quite exciting nonetheless. As was Tag when he'd arrived unexpectedly.

Smiling, Sam tried to pretend she wasn't overcome with the urge to cover her naked breasts.

"What's wrong?" Logan asked, looking at her expectantly.

"Nothing," she lied.

"Nothing?" Logan questioned, but then paused as he studied her. "So, you're gonna sit there and pretend that you don't wish you had clothes on?"

Sam laughed. This man knew her so well.

"Yes, I wish I had clothes on," she told him honestly.

"Why? You'd just have to take them off again."

True.

Sam smiled at him, flushed from her discomfiture. And it was true, she wished she had clothes on, but the unmistakable desire she saw in Logan's eyes made it more and more difficult to wish for anything more than sitting right there in front of him, completely exposed.

Much to her surprise, Logan began eating, sparing her a glance only every now and again. Although he made it look easy, she noticed the crease in his forehead, which was a telltale sign that he was having to focus extremely hard.

"God, this is good," he said, staring down at his plate as though seeing his food for the first time. "You made me lasagna."

"I did," she replied with a smile as she moved her food around on her plate. "How'd it go today?"

"Good. Although I learned that I still suck at golf."

"Well, it's a good thing you excel at other things," she said absently, looking up to meet his gaze.

"Think so?"

"I know so," she assured him.

Logan grinned but then turned his attention back to his plate as he continued to eat, pausing frequently to sip his wine.

If she wasn't mistaken, he was trying to distract himself from her nakedness. It didn't make things easier, but somehow, over the next half hour, Sam managed to make it through the meal, eating half of what was on her plate.

"You finished?" he asked nonchalantly, bringing her attention to him.

Glancing up, she realized he had pushed his plate away and was leaning back in his chair, his fingers sliding along the stem of his wineglass.

"Yes," she managed to say. Her breath was lodged in her throat, the longing in his gaze making her body tingle.

"Good."

Sam never knew what Logan was going to say or do next. Her husband was notorious for catching her off guard, and she had to assume that this was one of those times when he was going to do something she might question later.

"Stand up and come over here," he insisted, releasing his wineglass.

Doing as he instructed, Sam felt her face flame from embarrassment. It didn't matter that she was naked in front of this man often, or that there were times when she'd been naked in public, it never seemed to get any easier. Once she was on her feet, she stood before him, waiting.

"Turn around."

Sam turned around, facing away from him, her eyes closing as she tried to fight off the nerves.

When Logan's warm hands gripped her hips, Sam exhaled deeply. She loved the feel of his hands on her body. She wasn't sure she would ever get tired of his slightly roughened fingers caressing her.

His fingers played over her skin briefly before he cupped her bottom in both hands, gripping firmly. As he continued to knead with one hand, his other dipped between her legs, his finger sliding between her slick folds.

Sam moaned, the sensual invasion making her body tingle.

"Baby, you're wet."

Sam didn't respond because there was no reason to. And when he drove one long finger inside her, Sam thrust her hips backward instinctively, trying to drive him deeper.

"Such a beautiful ass," Logan said reverently. "I want to slide my dick right up inside of you, Sam."

Yes, she wanted that, too, and she was rapidly heading toward the pleading stage. Just when she thought he would add another finger to the first and fuck her into oblivion, he stopped.

"Please don't stop," she requested softly. She needed more, and it didn't matter that they were standing in the dining room and she was as naked as the day she was born.

"I don't plan to stop," he informed her. "But I do plan to move this out to the hot tub."

Okay. Good. She was good with that. The hot tub was definitely good.

And now she was mentally rambling just because he'd touched her.

"You go on out there, and I'll be there in just a second. No clothes, Sam."

Sam turned and looked up at him, trying to read his mind. What did he have planned?

Part of her was anxious, the other part merely curious. He was probably very aware of the heightened state she'd been in ever since she'd been introduced to Elijah Penn. Ever since the man had made his presence known by watching her so intently. Twice.

It'd been a major turn-on.

"Five minutes, that's all I need," he told her and turned her toward the door, swatting her bare butt to send her on her way.

With a shriek of laughter, Sam started moving. Faster than she'd thought possible.

# CHAPTER SEVEN

AFTER SAM MADE HER WAY OUTSIDE, LOGAN cleaned the kitchen. Not because he was stalling but because Sam had worked so hard to prepare a nice dinner, he wanted to ensure she wouldn't take on the chore of cleaning up.

Once that was finished, he discarded his shoes, grabbed two glasses and a bottle of wine, and made his way out to the hot tub, where his beautiful naked wife waited for him.

Naked.

Just like he'd asked her to be.

Honestly, Logan hadn't really expected her to be naked. And he certainly hadn't expected her to make him dinner. But again, the woman had surprised him. He loved when she did that.

As for what his original intentions had been when he'd made the suggestion earlier, he really hadn't had anything planned, other than to ravish her the way she deserved. Although, he had intended to keep her in suspense, especially since he'd had to eat dinner while she sat naked and patient across from him. That had been torture.

It had taken everything in him to keep from taking her right there on the table.

Yes, he wanted her that badly.

"Hi," she greeted when he joined her outside.

"Hi."

"Is that for me?"

Logan glanced down at the bottle of wine and then smiled at her. "That and more."

Sam laughed, a lyrical sound that he loved. "Well, what are you waiting for?"

Good question. What *was* he waiting for?

Setting the glasses and the bottle on the side of hot tub, Logan hurried out of his clothes, leaving them where they landed at his feet and then climbing into the tub of warm water. Before he made it all the way in, Sam had moved directly in front of him.

"What are you doing?" he asked, not needing an answer. He knew exactly what she was doing, and his dick was quickly rising to the occasion.

"Greeting you appropriately," she informed him, her wet hands sliding up his legs and then pushing his knees farther apart while he perched on the side of the tub. "Is that all right with you?"

"More than all right, baby."

Sam didn't waste any time before she took his cock into her mouth, long before her hands ever made it around him. She sucked him in deep, and he groaned while sliding his fingers through her silky hair.

"God, baby. I love when you do that." Boy, did he. The woman had a wicked mouth.

He kept his eyes fixed on her as she sucked him, her tongue teasing along the underside of his shaft while she looked up at him.

"Just like that," he instructed, holding her head firmly, pulling her closer. He had to fight to keep his ass planted on the ledge rather than thrusting forward, trying to drive his cock deeper.

Sam's soft moans sent vibrations along his cock, while her mouth worked him perfectly. "Slow down, baby," he told her, holding her hair more firmly when she began to bob her head in earnest. "I'm not ready to come just yet."

Hell, he wasn't ready to come at all. He'd much rather let her suck him for hours because it felt so damn good.

"Fuck, Sam. Your mouth feels good." He knew how much she liked when he talked to her.

Sam pulled her head back, still looking up at him, his cock falling from her mouth. "Tell me," she whispered.

"Tell you what?" he asked curiously.

"Like you did last night."

A surge of adrenaline caught fire inside of him as the memory of the night before rushed back. Sam had been fire in his arms after he'd started telling her exactly what he and Elijah would be doing to her the first chance they had. It was the second time he'd done it in the past week, and she'd ignited just as he'd expected.

"Did you have someone in mind?" he asked, feigning ignorance. He already knew the answer. From the moment that Elijah had walked into their playroom at Devotion, Logan had gotten the distinct impression that Sam was very interested in the man.

And truthfully, Logan was more than happy with her unabashed interest in Elijah.

Logan had talked to Elijah in depth just that afternoon. Although he'd had a brief email exchange with him that morning when Elijah asked about dinner, Logan had decided to call him on his way home from the golf course.

To make sure they were both on the same page.

They were.

And what he'd learned about Elijah had been very promising. Especially where Sam was concerned. The man wasn't shy about his intentions. That was a good thing, because Logan wasn't, either.

"Elijah," she mumbled now. Logan recognized what was most definitely concern in her pretty green eyes.

Forcing her back a little, he slid down into the hot water, his muscles singing with pleasure. Easing his way over to the reclining lounger, Logan pulled Sam with him. Once she was straddling him, he looked up at her.

"Does it bother you?" she asked suddenly.

"What? That you find Elijah attractive?" That was a given. Then again, the man was rather good-looking, even in Logan's very hetero opinion. The guy had class and elegance, all of the things that Sam seemed to find fascinating.

"That and..." She let the sentence trail off.

"That and you want him to join us?" Logan clarified.

"Do you not want that?"

When he started to answer her, Sam stopped him, her fingertips pressing against his lips.

"Listen to me for a minute, please."

Logan didn't try to speak, just nodded his head and watched her.

"I've been thinking about this for a long time. First, there was Luke and that was ... fun. I guess maybe *different* is a better word. You and Luke successfully introduced me to the side of myself that I didn't know existed."

Logan didn't interrupt, curious as to where she was going with this.

"And then Tag was there. Neither of them lasted long, and that was so long ago."

It had been a long time, Logan knew. They'd been refraining from playing like that for a while, mainly because Sam seemed to get attached and Logan hadn't been interested in something long-lasting with either man.

But what Logan had noticed throughout the entire time, neither of them had ever let up on their desire to have a third in their relationship. Which in turn had gotten him thinking. And perhaps Luke, Sierra, and Cole were on to something. Not that Logan had any interest in being with a man because ... well, he didn't. But that didn't mean that he and Sam couldn't venture into something that worked for them.

Something more permanent, because clearly, what they both sought was going to be life changing, no matter which way they looked at it.

Logan understood Sam's desire to have only one man involved in their relationship. It meant she was looking for long term, possibly even permanent. Logan had just never looked at it from her perspective before. Actually, he'd never looked much past the sex if he was completely honest. But now... Now he was seeing the possibility turning into something more.

He knew there were some permanent threesomes where the two men weren't interested in one another. That wasn't an issue, either. But Logan was a selfish bastard when it came to Sam's love. He wanted her to love him and only him. He didn't want to share that part of her with anyone.

And by being selfish, Logan was denying Sam. Denying her from finding what she truly needed. That's when he had started to wonder whether a permanent arrangement was going to be the only way for them to be able to continue to have what they'd found so long ago. What they both desperately wanted again.

"I won't lie," Sam told him now. "I like the threesomes. I would like for us to find that again."

"But you don't want temporary?" he asked, unable to keep the question to himself.

"No," she said honestly, her eyes curiously glassy. "If we're going to do this, I think we need to find something ... lasting."

He didn't say anything, needing her to clarify.

"I don't want to have random partners. I don't want to have to worry about getting attached to someone and them walking away from us. I don't think you want that, either."

No, he didn't. Too much risk.

"But I know you don't want a permanent person in our relationship, either."

"Do you?" Logan wasn't sure he wanted to know the answer to that question.

Sam's gaze darted away, and Logan pulled her chin with his finger, forcing her to look at him. "Tell me, Sam. Tell me exactly what you want."

"I'm scared," she admitted, and he noticed that the sheen in her eyes was unshed tears.

"About what?" God, Logan felt his stomach twist. Part anticipation, part fear.

"If I'm not mistaken, we get more out of a threesome than we do alone. Not," she said loudly, halting his argument, "that we have to have a threesome. It's just ... something we gravitate to. You and I both enjoy it."

Logan nodded. He didn't disagree. Although the two of them could burn the house to the ground with the combustible chemistry that arched between them, Logan did want something more. And he knew she craved it, as well.

"I think we're going to have to go a step further if we want something lasting. What we've done in the past just hasn't worked." Sam paused, her eyes locked with his. "Is that a bad thing?"

"No," he answered honestly. Logan had been thinking the same thing. At least since he'd met Elijah. For whatever reason, he felt as though there was a connection with Elijah. And it wasn't sexual on his part because he wasn't interested in men, but something in his gut told him this was going to be more.

To prove it, Logan had invited Elijah to play golf with them today. Elijah had kindly declined, letting him know that he had to fly to Florida and wouldn't be back until Sunday morning.

So, yeah, Logan was doing something he'd never done before, too. He was establishing a connection.

He'd already prepared himself for that. And after his conversation with Elijah that afternoon, he'd heard the unspoken request in the other man's tone. Elijah had fallen for Sam. Maybe not love at first sight, but likely damn near close. Elijah could do that, though, and never have to worry about letting go of Beth. Not only was Logan going to be sharing Sam with Elijah, Sam was going to be sharing Elijah with Beth.

"Is that still what you want? For us to include another man in the bedroom?"

Logan's throat constricted.

The bedroom.

God, they'd never had another man in their bed. Never. He wasn't sure he could do it now. That was the bed he shared with his wife.

"Are you asking me...?" Logan paused, swallowed. He didn't want to go there yet. Clearing his throat, he started again, "Are you asking me if I want to watch another man fuck you until you scream? If so, then yes. I want to feel you crushed between the two of us while I'm buried in your ass and he fucks your pussy." Logan was going to be very explicit. It was the only way he knew how to explain himself. "I want to watch you with a cock deep in your mouth while I'm buried in your pussy, pounding into you harder and harder."

His cock was back to full mast once again.

"But this is just sex for you?"

Logan heard the disappointment in her tone.

"No," he answered with ease. Much more so than he'd expected. "I understand what you need, Sam. I've never wanted a casual fling with anyone. You mean more to me than that. I don't want to share you with just anyone. If I'm going to share you with someone, I want it to be ... fulfilling."

"But you're scared I'm going to fall in love with someone else?"

Logan's heart twisted. The thought of Sam loving another man, it stole his breath.

"I... Fuck, Sam," he groaned, this time turning his eyes away from her.

"Talk to me," she pleaded, her voice soft. "We need to be on the same page, or we've got to do something different."

"Are you ready to fall in love with someone else?" he asked, his gut twisting painfully.

Sam cupped his cheeks and stared back at him. "I will never love another man the way that I love you. Never. I've never loved anyone the way that I love you. I'm not worried about that, and you shouldn't be, either."

Logan didn't miss the fact that she didn't deny that she could fall in love with someone else.

For now, he wasn't going to push the issue. It was a moot point, anyway, since they hadn't yet gotten to that place in their lives. If and when it happened, Logan would deal with it then. They would deal with it. Together.

"Sam," he said, wrapping his arms around her waist and pulling her closer. "God, help me, I still want it, but, more importantly, I want what makes you happy. I know you get attached, and I've learned to deal with that."

"But I still only love you," she said again.

"I know that." He hoped that, anyway. "I know you'll come to care about any person we're involved with. And I'm all right with that." Mostly.

He stared back at her, for the first time needing her confirmation more than he needed anything else. He wanted to truly believe that she wouldn't fall in love with another man, wouldn't want to invite another man permanently into their lives, but he knew how the heart worked. As much as he wished, he knew he couldn't have it both ways. The heart didn't react that way.

"I'm not interested in sharing my bed with another man, but I would like a commitment. Someone who isn't going to wander in and out of our lives so quickly," he added when she didn't say anything.

Logan had yet to inform her about Elijah's baggage, as Luke had referred to it. The man had a complex history. Logan didn't feel as though it was his place to share the details. He'd let Elijah talk to her, share that part of himself. But he could at least move forward tonight with the knowledge that Elijah just might be the man who could help fulfill their fantasies even if he did present some complications.

"We're on the same page, baby," he said, pulling her head down until their lips met. "I want the same thing. I want to watch you come a million different ways. I want to watch while he buries his tongue in your pussy, teasing your clit while I slide my cock in and out of your mouth." Logan thrust his tongue into her mouth, mimicking the motion of what he'd love to do with his cock. He didn't let up until Sam was moaning and clinging to him.

For now, he would distract her, remind her exactly what he could do to her body, how hot he could make her. And vice versa.

Because they were okay. They were always going to be okay. If two people could make this work, it would be them.

So for tonight, he'd be the one filling her, making her scream. And tomorrow, they'd worry about Elijah.

# CHAPTER EIGHT

ELIJAH MADE HIS WAY THROUGH THE RESTAURANT promptly at seven o'clock, just as he and Logan had agreed. That foreign rush of emotion surged once again the moment he set eyes on Samantha from across the crowded room. It was only foreign because, until recently, he hadn't felt it in ... well, in years.

Winding his way through the other tables, Elijah approached the table in the back where Samantha and Logan were sitting, and as he approached, Logan stood, showing his impeccable manners, which was something Elijah admired in the man.

The two men shook hands, and then Elijah turned his attention to Samantha, taking her hand and bringing it to his lips as he leaned down. "It's a pleasure to see you again," he whispered to her, enjoying the way her eyes glazed over.

This woman was remarkable.

Once he was seated on Samantha's right, their waiter approached, reading off the wine list when Logan inquired. Their selection was made, their glasses poured, and the three of them were left alone while they reviewed the menu.

Another few minutes had passed before the waiter returned to take their order, and during that time, Elijah felt Samantha's eyes on him frequently. He fought the urge to smile or to meet Sam's inquiring gaze.

Although her husband sat on her left, for some uncanny reason, Elijah appreciated the attention Samantha was showing him. It wasn't awkward, and surprisingly it didn't even feel like betrayal.

When Elijah glanced up from the menu he'd been perusing, he noticed Logan was looking at him. Their eyes met briefly, but what he saw reflecting back at him wasn't anger or concern, or jealousy, for that matter. It almost seemed like acceptance.

Apparently, Elijah's candid chat yesterday had gotten through to Logan.

*"I'm not interested in a one-night stand, Logan. I'll be frank with you. Meeting Samantha, I didn't quite expect her to have such an effect on me. Since the first time I saw her, I haven't thought of anything but her. Do you understand what I'm telling you?"*

*"I understand."*

*"I'm not sure you do. I panicked because of her effect on me. And yes, I hauled ass because it scared the shit out of me. You've already reprimanded me for my actions, and I listened to you. It's your turn. You need to listen to me. Logan, if this is not something that you can handle, we need to part ways now. I would never approach Samantha in the way I want to without your blessing. I understand what this is. I accept it. I just want you to know up front that I don't want one night. And I'm not looking for temporary."*

By the end of that phone call, Elijah had felt immensely better. And he got the feeling Logan had, as well. Elijah had ended the call by suggesting Logan have a heart-to-heart with his wife because what they were about to embark upon was going to test boundaries of all kinds.

The fact that Logan and Samantha were there with him now told Elijah that they were all in agreement.

At least so far.

Once their orders were placed, Elijah allowed himself to admire Samantha a little more. She looked radiant in her off-white silk blouse and prim black skirt. The woman exuded class, which he found exceptionally desirable.

"So, tell me how the two of you met," he prompted Samantha when the silence descended on the table.

The way Samantha's eyes lit up as she glanced over at Logan spoke volumes. The woman was totally in love with her husband, and Elijah felt more at ease instantly. These two had a connection that was often missing from some, for lack of a better term, open relationships. He'd seen it a time or two during his interactions at the clubs.

He knew that Samantha and Logan didn't have an open marriage because what they opted to do was to bring a third person into the mix. According to Logan, neither of them was looking for something *outside* of their marriage. Elijah respected that immensely. It said a lot about Logan that he would come out and speak so candidly about what he did and didn't want in a polyamorous relationship. Not all people did that. Then again, Elijah was under the impression that Logan and Samantha were looking to take this to a whole new level. At least compared to what they'd had before.

Elijah understood quite clearly.

"I'm originally from San Antonio, born and raised, and my parents and my brother are still there. I was working at one of the remote branches of XTX when a position came open at their main offices here in Dallas. At the request of my boss at the time, I interviewed for a position, and Logan was the one to interview me," Sam admitted, picking up her wineglass.

"That sounds scandalous," Elijah smiled. And interesting. He already knew the backstory, thanks to his many conversations with Logan, but he knew there were always two sides to every story.

Sam laughed, and the woman's voice was sexy, as was her confidence as she sat facing him directly. "It wasn't intentional, I assure you. I couldn't resist him, though."

Logan laughed, and Elijah looked over at him, smiling as he waited for the rest of the story.

"I think it was the other way around."

"Okay, so maybe it took me a little while to get with the program," Sam said, glancing back and forth between Elijah and Logan. "But once I did, I can say my life changed entirely."

"So, I take it you got the job."

"I'll say," she laughed, that sensual sound causing Elijah to watch her closely.

There was no doubt about it; he was intrigued by this woman.

"And how did he change your life? Aside from the obvious," Elijah said, glancing down at the rock on Samantha's left hand. Beneath the table, Elijah fingered his own wedding ring.

"He awakened a part of me I didn't know existed," Sam stated seriously, and Elijah decided right then that he liked Samantha even more. The woman was straight to the point. None of the fumbling or giggling that Elijah heard often from women.

"I can only presume you mean sexually?" he asked.

Samantha paused and glanced around before answering, apparently looking to see if anyone was within hearing distance. Elijah already knew that no one was, but he appreciated Sam's need to be discreet in her response.

"Both sexually and emotionally."

Interesting answer. Elijah didn't immediately ask a question, and he wasn't very surprised when Samantha threw out one of her own.

"I noticed you're wearing a ring."

Elijah didn't try to deny it, although said ring was currently beneath the table so Sam obviously hadn't just noticed it.

He had known the question would come about at some point. "I am ... yes," he told her softly as he placed his hand on the table, twisting the wedding band on his left hand. He still wore it. Even all these years later.

As soon as it registered exactly what he'd said, Samantha's eyes darted down toward his left hand. Instantly, her body language changed and she looked ... upset.

When she finally met his gaze again, Elijah continued, "My Beth passed away four years ago. Brain cancer."

Her entire demeanor softened and she leaned forward. "Oh, Elijah, I'm so sorry for your loss," Samantha said, reaching for his hand.

Elijah liked the way her hand felt when she touched him. Soft, smooth fingers. He glanced down where their hands met and then back up at her. He didn't respond to her; nothing needed to be said.

She didn't pull her hand away as she added, "If you don't mind me asking, how did the two of you meet?"

Elijah smiled. Yes, Samantha McCoy continued to surprise him. Most people shied away from talking about his wife once he told them that she was dead. Probably out of fear that he would break down in front of them. That wasn't going to happen. He loved talking about Beth. She was a significant part of his life; she was the woman who had made him who he was today.

And he reserved the breaking down part for when he was alone.

"I was attending a trade show, as a vendor, and I happened to run into her. I didn't know it at the time, but she'd been the one to put the show together, with the help of several other people. Beth was an event planner. She was one of those people who was meticulous about details. When she caught my eye, she'd been ensuring everything was going exactly as intended. It took me a few tries, but I finally found the nerve to ask her out. She said yes. The rest is history."

"How long were the two of you married?" Sam asked.

"It'll be thirteen years this month," Elijah said, noticing that when Logan's hand disappeared beneath the table, Samantha retrieved her hand from his. "We dated for three years before I found the right time to propose. We lived together for two years before we were finally married."

Which meant he'd been married to her for almost eight years before she passed away, but as far as Elijah was concerned, Beth was it for him. Even without her there every single day, he still thought about her. Still loved her with every breath he took. And he knew without a doubt that there would never be another woman to take her place.

When the waiter interrupted to bring salads, the table quieted, and Elijah couldn't help but wonder whether he'd darkened the mood at the table. A minute or two later, Samantha's gaze aligned with his, and he saw that she didn't seem at all bothered by their topic of discussion. No, now she just looked curious.

"So, can I ask a personal question?" Samantha asked as they ate.

Elijah paused, his salad fork resting against his plate. "Of course."

"Have you ever done this before?"

Well, that was about as personal as any question could get. Not that Elijah minded, because he received that question quite frequently. He interacted with many people who shared the same lifestyle that he did and because of how taboo some people felt it was, there were often inquisitions into how many polyamorous relationships he'd been a part of.

"My official answer to that is yes," he said easily. "If you're asking how many threesomes I've interacted with, it has been several. However, I assure you that I've always been safe."

"Only one of them was permanent?"

"I'm not sure I'd call it permanent. More like long term. Beth had believed it was forever."

"You were in a threesome with your wife?" Sam asked, sounding surprised.

"My wife and my best friend, James. Why? Did you think this was something I came up with recently?"

"I'm sorry, I didn't mean to assume," Sam answered, glancing down.

Elijah reached over and lifted her chin with his finger. "I don't mind answering questions," he told her. "This is an important topic." Considering. "So, yes, technically, I've only been in a long-term polyamorous relationship once. It unfortunately came to an end when Beth got sick."

Sam's eyes were shiny, her emotions right there for anyone to see. Elijah found that endearing.

Elijah decided to steer the conversation back toward Samantha for now. He didn't want to be an emotional drain on her tonight. He had a lot of baggage, he knew it, and from the looks of it, Samantha and Logan knew it, too. There would be a better time and place to talk about all of the details later. "And how about you? How many threesomes have you been a part of?"

Elijah waited for Samantha to answer, knowing full well what the answer was. He'd already questioned Logan about this exact subject. Considering Logan had approached him, Elijah had been curious as to what Logan and Sam were interested in. What their intentions were.

"Two..." Sam hesitated.

"Only two?" he asked, setting his fork down on his salad plate and pushing it away.

"Yes. I didn't engage in this sort of activity prior to meeting Logan. And since we got together," she explained, glancing over at Logan briefly, "there have been two men who I was involved with."

"And you enjoy that sort of interaction?"

"Yes." Samantha's straightforward answer made Elijah smile.

"And you're looking to find a more permanent — as you referred to it — person to be involved with?"

The hesitation that followed was the answer Elijah was looking for. Samantha might know what she wanted, but as to how she was to go about asking for it, she still appeared confused.

Based on what he understood, Samantha enjoyed threesomes; however, she seemed to establish attachments to the men she was with. For Logan, he wasn't looking for temporary. Not that he seemed interested in permanent, but the man was looking for something more. That he was certain of.

Elijah was happy to say, he believed he could offer them both what they wanted. And in return, he'd get what he needed.

# CHAPTER NINE

SAM STARED BACK AT ELIJAH, WONDERING HOW she should answer the question. Truth be told, she'd already started to see where Elijah was going with the conversation, and she couldn't help but realize exactly what the man was implying.

Glancing over at Logan, then back to Elijah, Samantha opted for the truth. "At the risk of making this sound like a job interview," Sam told him with a laugh, "I'm not looking for a one-night stand. I don't care for temporary or fleeting, either. We've done that already, and as you can imagine, it isn't easy for me."

Sam noticed the way Elijah's eyes darted to Logan and then back to her. "Then I'm happy to say that the three of us seem to be on the same page," Elijah said, and a bolt of heat erupted in Sam's core. "In fact, I informed Logan yesterday pretty much the same thing."

Sam kept her eyes on Elijah, seeing the heat reflected in his intense gaze. The man was mouthwatering. He reminded her a lot of Logan in the way he carried and presented himself.

He was a businessman, first and foremost. And it was clear that he put a lot of effort — and money — into his appearance with the expensive suits he wore. Not that the money mattered to her in the least, but the effort certainly did. His hair was a dark chocolate brown, his eyes were honey gold. He had a chiseled jaw, his nose was just a little too big but somehow perfect on his face, and his thick eyelashes probably made a million women jealous.

And of course, there was that GQ stubble and the slightly unkempt hair that made her want to reach out and touch him just to feel the rasp of his beard and the silky softness of his hair.

He was incredibly handsome; there was no doubt about it.

"What's your favorite color?" she asked bluntly, suddenly anxious to know everything there was to know about this man.

"Blue," he answered without hesitation.

"Do you have any brothers or sisters?"

"One sister; she's almost fifteen years younger than I am. Yes, she was planned. My parents started early with me. Really early. They had me before they graduated from high school."

"Wow," Sam said, speechless. "Sorry, not *that* sort of wow. I'm just... That's interesting. I'd love to meet your mother."

Logan chuckled and Sam looked over at him. Her husband seemed to be enjoying this discussion.

"How about we make a deal?" Elijah stated, catching her attention again. When she made eye contact, he continued. "For every question you ask me, I get to ask you one in return."

Sam loved his accent and the sexy cadence of his voice. It was smooth and rich, with a hint of raspy mixed in. "All right," she agreed, realizing too late what she'd just agreed to.

"Do you like to be spanked?" Elijah asked, and the deep baritone mixed with the question he was asking sent a shiver down Sam's spine.

"Not particularly." Sam remembered the time Logan had spanked her, and yes, she had enjoyed it, but that had been different. He hadn't been intending to cause her pain. That had been the day Tag had waltzed into her life and turned their twosome back into a threesome.

"Very well."

It was her turn again. "Do you belong to any other clubs besides Devotion?"

"No. Not now, anyway. I was a member of a polyamory club, but I recently left of my own accord. Most of the members were in a committed relationship, and those who weren't generally wanted one night of fun. I grew tired of that quickly."

Sam didn't even have a chance to process his answer before he was asking another question. "Do you like to be blindfolded?"

Sam felt her cheeks heat and knew she was probably turning bright red. Instinctively, she turned and looked at Logan, who merely shrugged. He had informed her before they'd arrived that he wouldn't be answering her questions for her. If she wanted to establish a relationship with Elijah, she had to make him feel comfortable with her. As Logan had put it, Elijah wasn't interested in him; he was interested in her, which meant Sam would be Elijah's sole focus. Sam understood that, but it didn't make the questions any easier.

"Yes," she choked out, grabbing her wineglass and downing the rest. She noticed the smirk on Elijah's mouth, and she forced herself to look away.

Suddenly, Elijah's smooth fingers were on her bare thigh, and Sam felt the air rush from her lungs. His touch, although unexpected, was incredibly gentle, yet firm. Completely different from Logan's slightly rough touch. Elijah's hands were much smoother against her skin, and Sam was suddenly motionless, her body absorbing the feel of those soft fingers.

"I only have one request, Sam."

"What's that?" Sam managed to say the words although there was no air in her lungs. Elijah's fingers were gently brushing up her leg, sliding over her inner thigh.

"I expect complete honesty from you. I want to know what you like, what you don't like. And more importantly, I want to get to know you a lot more."

Sam hadn't expected them to get quite so personal so quickly tonight. But she understood, so she nodded, unable to find her voice.

And just like that, Elijah's hand was gone, and Sam felt slightly ashamed because she immediately wished for it to be back.

When the waiter approached with their food a few minutes later, Sam welcomed the distraction. She needed a minute.

Or hell, maybe ten.

---

ALL THROUGH DINNER, LOGAN SAT QUIETLY, ADDING his comments only when necessary, but mostly taking in the dynamic at the table. Most of the interaction was between Sam and Elijah, and he had to admit, he was rather impressed. By both of them.

Not often did Samantha engage in such personal conversation with practical strangers, but she was opening up nicely to Elijah. Whether they were talking about business or sex, the two of them never wavered in their responses. The topics continued to border on intimately personal, at least as much as Sam was willing to discuss in a public setting such as this one, but she was holding her own.

Logan could tell that Elijah was impressed. Or perhaps enamored was a better word for it. He could see the lust burning in Elijah's eyes. The man wanted Sam. And it was a fucking turn-on to watch.

There was unquestionably attraction on his part, but Logan couldn't blame the guy. Sam was a remarkable sight, that was for sure. She'd managed to catch his attention from the second he'd laid eyes on her on his computer monitor during a video conference call, and even after all this time, Logan was just as intrigued by her.

Now that dinner was finished, dessert passed up, and coffee being savored, Logan had to wonder what was going to happen next. His original plan had been to take Sam to Devotion, but based on the fire kindling right there at the table, he was beginning to think somewhere a little more private was in order.

A few minutes later, it was clear they were finished and ready to move on to something else. He just wasn't sure what that was at the moment.

Logan didn't have a chance to pick up the check because apparently Elijah had taken care of that beforehand. Or so he'd been told when Logan had excused himself from the table and approached the waiter directly. He'd have to hand it to the guy; Elijah knew how to take care of everything.

He had to confess to watching Elijah with genuine interest for some time during the night. The man was refined and extremely confident, making it difficult not to pay attention to him. He didn't appear to be playing games with Sam. Instead, he was straightforward with both his questions and his answers. He didn't stumble with his answers, didn't insert filler words at any time, and he didn't fidget.

He'd been completely up front with Sam, and the only time Logan saw Sam falter was when Elijah touched her. Hell, he had faltered himself. Not that he could see what Elijah was doing, but based on the expression on Sam's face, he knew that his wife had been enjoying his touch.

"What do you say we get out of here?" Logan asked, wanting to get this moving. He didn't care one way or the other if Sam decided not to take things to the next level tonight, but he did want to know which direction they would be headed.

"I think that's a wonderful suggestion," Elijah added, glancing over at Logan. He got the sense that Elijah was used to making all of the decisions.

"I know we had planned to go to Devotion," Sam stated, glancing between the two of them. "But I was wondering if maybe we could go somewhere else."

"Did you have somewhere in mind?" Elijah asked.

"Our house," she said quickly, her voice quivering with what Logan assumed was nerves.

It was the question of the hour. Based on the fact that Sam asked, Logan knew she was still interested.

"I would love to," Elijah said softly as he glanced between the two of them.

That was Logan's cue. If he were in agreement, he would stand. So he did. As did Elijah. They both waited for Samantha to rise. The three of them headed toward the door, Elijah leading the way.

"You good with this?" Logan whispered to Sam as they stepped out into the warm evening air.

Her quick smile was her only answer, and Logan took her hand. Elijah said a quick good-bye, informing them he'd see them at their house shortly as Logan handed the ticket to the valet. While they waited, Logan texted Elijah their address so he could get directions on his phone, per his request.

A few minutes later, Logan was pulling away from the curb, heading home.

"Are you really okay with this?" Sam mumbled as she sat quietly in the passenger's seat.

Logan glanced over at her as he reached for her hand. Their fingers linked, and he returned his focus to driving.

"Sam, if I had any doubts whatsoever, I wouldn't have introduced you to Elijah. I like the guy. I think he's a good man. Am I hesitant? Sure. A little. Do I want to see him fuck you crazy? Yeah, I fucking do." That was no less than the truth. "I'm not trying to think this to death. I don't want you to, either."

It was more than obvious that Sam liked Elijah. On a level that was more than sex. Honestly, Logan wasn't sure what he thought of that. If he said he wasn't interested in seeing what might happen between the two them, he'd be lying. It had been a long time since they'd invited a third to their bed, so to speak. He was looking forward to it more than he was even letting on, though. The idea of the man buried inside of Sam's pussy while Logan fucked her ass was something he'd thought about plenty in recent days.

It had been a year and a half since they'd engaged in any activity involving a third person. The last one had been Tag, and Logan knew how much that had cost Sam. She'd been devastated when Tag had opted to move on. Sure, Sam was happy for him and McKenna, but Logan knew she'd been a bit attached.

That was the main reason he liked Elijah. The notion of a man who was looking for something more than just a good time but not looking for something as permanent as marriage seemed like the answer to their prayers. They didn't have to worry about him moving on — or at least Logan didn't think they did.

"I do find him incredibly attractive," Sam stated, drawing Logan's attention from the road momentarily. When he glanced over, he found her staring at him. "But I find you sexy as hell."

Logan grinned.

Sam's fingers squeezed his and she held his hand tightly as they drove home.

"Are you sure you want to do this?" he questioned again.

"Yes, I do. I definitely do."

"Are you worried about something?"

There was a brief pause before Sam answered, which worried Logan. "I'm just nervous, I guess. I don't want to get involved with someone who might move on quickly. Do you think we should be worried about that with him?" she asked, and Logan could feel her gaze on him.

"Were you worried about it the last time?"

"No, I guess not."

Logan didn't say anything because he could tell Sam had more to add.

"Okay, so maybe I was a little worried. At first. I thought Tag was going to be around for a little longer than he was."

"Well, the only thing we can do is take it one day at a time, baby. You know that."

"I do know that."

Truthfully, Logan really didn't think they'd have to worry about Elijah moving on. In fact, he was thinking just the opposite. Elijah was interested in Sam. In more than just sex, and he knew that. It was evident in the way the man looked at her, interacted with her. Even though Logan had been right there with them, there were times when it'd seemed as though he was on the outside looking in. Which wasn't necessarily a bad thing.

He just had to figure out whether or not he was willing to share all of her. He was doing his damnedest not to be selfish. He didn't mind sharing her body, as long as she was game, but he was scared to share her heart.

He could only hope that they had accomplished what they'd set out to by going to dinner tonight. Expectations were set and everyone seemed to be congruent. He didn't doubt for one minute that Elijah would let Sam see the real him, but he could only hope that Elijah didn't fall in love with Sam the same way Logan had.

A few minutes later, they were pulling into their driveway. There weren't any cars parked along the street, which meant Elijah wasn't there yet.

Once Logan pulled into the garage, parked, and turned the car off, the garage door closing behind them, he angled so he could face Sam.

"Remember that night when I brought you back to my place and had you get naked right here in this car?"

Sam nodded, her eyes widening.

"Were you scared that night?"

"Yes," she whispered. "In a good way."

Logan grinned. "I hope you feel the same about tonight. Let me be in charge. I swear to you, Sam. I'll take care of you."

"I know you will," she uttered with conviction.

"Then, baby, it's time for you to let me take control. From this point onward, you'll do exactly what I tell you to. Understand?"

"Yes."

God, he loved the husky sound of her voice when she was turned on.

"Good, then let me take care of you tonight. Starting right now."

# CHAPTER TEN

ELIJAH PURPOSELY TOOK HIS TIME GETTING TO Logan and Sam's house. As soon as he'd received Logan's text with their address, he'd keyed the information into his navigation, but he hadn't left the restaurant parking lot right away.

Instead, he'd sat right there, in the front seat of his car, and stared out into the dark night that had consumed the city while they'd been having dinner.

But now he was sitting out in front of Logan's house, patiently waiting. For what? He had no idea.

Okay, so maybe he was trying to steel his nerves just a little. This was a huge step for him. And it had nothing to do with the fact that he was going to go inside and find himself falling into bed with a married woman.

No, he suspected there might be a different sort of falling going on.

"Beth, honey, please give me the strength to make it through the night without totally losing myself."

He'd never asked that of her before. Then again, he'd never met Samantha McCoy until recently.

Elijah didn't fear that he would fall in love with a woman who would make him forget Beth. That wasn't possible. However, until Samantha, Elijah hadn't expected to meet a woman who would captivate him in ways only Beth had been able to do.

But tonight at dinner, he'd found himself completely enraptured by Samantha. The way she spoke, the way she moved ... especially the way she looked at him.

She made him feel as though he weren't just a third wheel. She made him believe that she wanted something more than just a roll in the sheets. Not to mention, he got a good vibe from Logan. The man wasn't just interested in watching some random man fuck his wife. No, this was ... strange to say, but it seemed serious for the two of them.

That was refreshing. And profoundly different from what he had originally expected.

And he got the distinct impression that Logan knew it, too.

But the man hadn't bugged off. He hadn't tried to disengage or change the subject. In fact, he'd pretty much left him and Sam alone at dinner, offering them a chance to get to know one another on a more personal level.

That might've been the biggest mistake of all, because Elijah felt a connection to Samantha. It scared the shit out of him, but it settled something inside of him that hadn't been at peace since the day Beth had taken her last breath.

He wasn't waiting for Beth to answer him. He knew that wasn't going to happen, but he did trust his gut. If he weren't supposed to be there, he would know it.

For whatever reason, Logan had entrusted Samantha to him. And now it was time to see where this was going to go.

Maybe it would be just one night, regardless of what they'd all stated up front. Maybe it would turn into a night full of incredible sex and mind-blowing experiences. And then in a few hours, or hell, even tomorrow morning, he would walk out of their house and move on with his life. They would, as well.

Or this could be a pivotal point in which Elijah found that missing piece that could very well keep him together for what was left of his natural life.

Shit. When the hell had he gotten so damned sentimental?

*When it became clear you were going to spend the rest of your life alone, you idiot.*

Quieting the internal monologue, he forced open the car door and planted his feet firmly on the ground before pushing himself out of the car. He stood there for a moment, glancing up at the stars as though the answer might be written right there somewhere between the Big Dipper and the North Star.

No. There weren't any answers, but again, he went with his gut.

He was supposed to be there.

A minute later, Elijah was knocking gently on the front door. He didn't have to wait long before Logan was there, opening the door and stepping back so he could come inside.

"Sam's waiting for you," Logan said, not a hint of unease in his tone.

"For me?"

"Well, technically for us. But I can assure you she's anticipating your arrival."

As the door closed behind him, Elijah turned to face Logan, searching the other man's face for signs that this wasn't what he wanted.

What he saw positively wasn't uncertainty etched into the hard angles of Logan's face.

"She's nervous," Logan told him. "But it's the good kind."

Elijah laughed. "I didn't know there was a good kind."

"With her there is."

Elijah nodded and then fell into step behind Logan as he was led through the house.

"Drink?"

"Sure," Elijah answered. "I'll have what you're having."

Elijah noticed a bottle of Hpnotiq sitting on the counter near the stainless steel refrigerator. "Very nice," he told Logan.

"This happens to be one of Sam's favorites. I introduced her to it in Vegas a couple of years ago."

"Good to know."

Elijah watched as Logan prepared the drinks and then handed him one before motioning with his raised glass toward a set of double doors at the back of the room. "She's waiting outside for us."

Not wanting to lead the way, Elijah took a step back and then followed Logan. When they walked out onto the veranda, the first thing Elijah noticed was the exquisite woman sitting on a lounge chair, completely and gloriously naked. Well, almost completely. Samantha wore a narrow strip of black fabric over her eyes.

His heart skipped a beat. Literally.

Logan didn't speak, just nodded toward Elijah, and words weren't necessary. As he continued to look at Sam, Elijah wasn't sure he'd be able to make his tongue work, so he welcomed the silence.

Logan motioned him toward one of the chairs sitting at the end of the lounge chair, just a foot or so away. When Logan took a seat in the other, Elijah followed his lead, lowering himself into the chair, sipping the blue-tinged vodka that held a hint of fruit juice. He was more of a scotch man, but this worked for tonight. Especially if it gave him more insight into Samantha.

"Pretty, isn't she?" Logan asked, and Elijah watched as Sam's muscles tensed slightly.

She was blindfolded — something, yes, she did appear fond of — so clearly she couldn't see either of them.

"Flawless," Elijah said.

Sam's full pink lips tilted slightly, as did her head, as she seemed to follow the sound of his voice.

"Spread your legs Sam," Logan told her, and Sam did exactly as she was told, her legs opening to give Elijah an unobstructed view of her bare mound and the pretty pink flesh between.

Elijah sucked in a breath. As he nearly drooled over her lovely form, he noticed that Sam's hands were trembling ever so slightly.

"I guess we won't be talking this through," Sam stated, but Elijah heard the teasing in her voice.

"Do we need to discuss this further?" he asked, just to placate her.

"Not unless you need to," she responded, her words soft, concerned.

"I'm quite content, thank you. This view is perfect." Elijah paused. "This *night* is perfect."

Logan sipped his drink, not saying a word, so Elijah did the same. He didn't look away from Sam, admiring every single inch of her beautiful body.

She had a lot of curves, softly rounded. Not too skinny, either, something Elijah very much appreciated. Her firm breasts were tipped with dusky pink nipples, and they were currently beaded from her arousal.

"Did you have trouble finding the place?" Logan asked casually.

"Not at all."

"Do you live close by?"

"Not very far. About ten minutes," Elijah said, taking another sip of his drink. Glancing over at Logan, Elijah opted for a question of his own. "Does she taste as good as she looks?"

"She does. Perfection through and through," Logan offered.

Elijah didn't doubt it, either.

A minute later, Logan stood from his chair after setting his empty glass on the concrete. Elijah divided his attention between Sam and Logan, not in a rush. He was pleasantly relaxed sitting there, watching this incredible woman. Her chest had begun to rise and fall rapidly, her lust evident.

"Sit up," Logan said gently, speaking to Sam.

She did, and Logan eased in behind her, fully clothed while his wife was naked. He seemed very much in control of the situation, which also put Elijah at ease.

"Elijah is watching you, baby," Logan whispered against Sam's ear, loud enough for Elijah to hear clearly. "Just like he did at Devotion. Does that turn you on?"

Elijah watched as Logan slipped one hand down between Sam's thighs, his fingers separating her folds and exposing her soft, pink pussy.

"Yes," she breathed.

"Do you want him to watch while I finger your pussy?" Logan asked.

"Yes."

"Like this?" Logan asked as he dipped one finger inside of his wife.

Elijah's cock was hard, confined behind the zipper of his pants. He was tempted to ease himself by stroking the rigid erection through his slacks but decided to hold off. This was getting better by the second.

"So wet," Logan groaned. "Taste yourself on my finger, Sam."

While Elijah sat transfixed on the sight, Logan lifted one glistening finger up to Sam's mouth, and her little pink tongue came out and lapped over the tip. Elijah groaned, unable to help himself.

"You hear that? That was just for you," Logan told Sam. "And you feel this?" Logan reached behind her back, presumably adjusting himself.

"Yes," Sam said on a breathy moan.

"That's just for you, too. I can't wait to slide into your sweet body, Sam. And I want to watch while you suck Elijah's cock deep into your mouth."

Sam groaned at the same time Elijah did.

Yeah, it was clear; this was going to be a good night.

# CHAPTER ELEVEN

SAM COULD HARDLY BREATHE; HER HEART POUNDED from the excitement of knowing Elijah was watching her while Logan held her close, his heavy arms comforting her.

The night air was warm, Logan's body even warmer, and the tingle that had erupted in her core only worked to heat her from the inside out.

Sam had long ago lost all concern about being outside, where anyone could see them. And she'd seemingly lost the anxiety where Elijah was concerned, as well. In fact, at the moment, she just wanted to touch him.

Logan must've known that, too, because he leaned in close to her ear and whispered, this time for only her to hear, "Last time I'll ask this. Is this what you want?"

"I do," she confirmed. More than anything.

Logan pressed a kiss to her neck, just beneath her ear. "I love you, Sam."

Warmth consumed her, more so than any physical heat could have. The sound of his voice, the reassurance in his tone, it meant more to her than anything else. And now, they were moving into very dangerous territory, one that threatened to test them, but Sam didn't have any fear. Not when it came to Logan's love.

"I love you, too," she replied. "More than you'll ever know."

Her love for Logan was unbreakable. Even if she felt she was going to fall for Elijah in a way she hadn't anticipated.

Ever since dinner ... ever since the man had pulled her in and charmed her with his enchanting smile, his sexy accent, and the impassioned look she'd seen in his golden eyes. He wanted her. That was something she knew for a fact. But she also got the impression that he wanted more than just tonight.

That didn't bother her. Although she had worried that it would bother Logan when he figured it out. That was until she realized the two men had laid it all on the line. This, according to Elijah, wasn't his first time doing this, as he'd told her at dinner. And from her perspective, that dinner had actually been their first date, one that Sam wasn't sure she'd ever forget.

"Oh, God," Sam moaned when Logan slowly pushed his finger back inside of her. He was just teasing her now, but the fact that she was blindfolded had heightened her other senses, making it significantly more effective.

"Very pretty," Elijah said, his voice carrying from wherever he sat. Sam could tell he was close, but not close enough. At least not close enough for her to touch him.

"Yes, she is," Logan confirmed against her ear, his breath tickling her neck. "So fucking pretty."

God, she loved when he talked to her like that. The gentle rumble of his deep voice sent a shiver racing along her nerve endings, lighting them up along the way.

"I want you to move to the end of the chair," Logan instructed softly. "I'll be right here behind you."

Sam eased forward until she felt the end of the chair against her thighs. Logan positioned his hands on her hips, halting her.

"Stand up," Logan instructed, but based on the way he was still holding her, Sam knew he wasn't speaking to her.

Although Logan appeared to be the one in control, Sam detected a request in Logan's tone, versus his usual commanding manner.

That's the moment she knew this was different.

Very, very different.

---

LOGAN WATCHED AS ELIJAH PUSHED TO HIS feet. He'd placed his half-empty glass on the concrete beside his chair, his eyes still trained on Samantha. The man was enraptured by her, Logan could tell. Not that he blamed the guy.

It was one of the signals that told him this was different from their previous threesomes. With Luke, it had been about sex. Logan's twin had been there for the gratification only, to do to Sam what Logan requested, and they'd all known it. And with Tag, it had been the same.

Nothing complicated.

If Logan had to guess, Elijah had already fallen for Sam, even if he didn't know it yet. Then again, maybe he did, because he moved forward, his hands coming to cradle Sam's head, sliding down until he was cupping her face. She was looking up at him, not seeing him due to the blindfold, but from where Logan sat, even she was aware of their acknowledgement of one another.

"Is this what you want, Samantha?" Elijah asked, his hands cupping her face gently. "I need to hear you say it."

"Yes, this is what I want," Sam whispered. "I want both of you."

Elijah's eyes met Logan's over the top of Sam's head. Logan waited to see what the man would say. He could tell there was a battle going on in his head. This wasn't just physical for Elijah. That was evident.

And for reasons unbeknownst to him, Logan was all right with that. This man would care for Sam the way she deserved. The way Logan cared for her. If he was going to share more of her than her body, Logan needed to know that he would take care of her.

Elijah finally nodded, an obvious signal that he was ready to move forward.

Logan slid his hands down Sam's arms and then took her wrists as he lifted them, placing her hands on the front of Elijah's slacks, just above the stiff ridge of his erection. "Take his pants off, Sam."

Sam's fingers fumbled only briefly, as she unhooked Elijah's belt, then freed the button and lowered the zipper. While she was doing that, Elijah watched her. When she'd freed him, Elijah then shrugged out of his suit jacket and tossed it on the chair behind him.

Elijah didn't need instruction, nor did Sam. Logan sat there, his hands sliding up and down Sam's smooth thighs, lingering between her legs as Elijah undressed himself, with minimal help from Sam. When he was fully nude, standing just a few inches from Sam, Logan glanced back up at him.

And he nodded.

This was a joint effort tonight. Logan didn't want to be the one directing it. There was a strange intimacy that he'd never felt before, and he knew that by taking control, he'd ruin that for all of them.

"Touch me, Sam," Elijah groaned, his hands circling his thick cock.

Sam's pale hands slid up Elijah's toned thighs, but she didn't go right for his cock. She seemed to be feeling her way, literally and figuratively. Her hands caressed his skin slowly, moving up to his hips, over his washboard abs, then back down.

"Just like that," Elijah encouraged. "Your hands are so soft."

Logan heard the catch in Elijah's words. He hadn't taken his eyes off Sam, and he was clearly lost in the moment.

Sliding Sam's hair over her shoulder, Logan leaned down and pressed his lips to her neck, sucking gently as he cupped her breasts with his hands, teasing her nipples with his fingertips. When she moaned, he closed his eyes briefly.

He continued to press kisses along her shoulders, up each side of her neck, until she was squirming in his hands, pressing her chest forward as he gently kneaded her breasts.

"You're so beautiful, Samantha," Elijah said, his hands sliding over hers where they rested on his thighs. Logan watched unabashedly as Elijah directed her to where he wanted her. When she'd wrapped her pale fingers around the heavy stalk of flesh standing at full attention, Sam groaned. As did Elijah.

"Oh, fuck," Elijah growled, his thigh muscles flexing. Logan figured he was trying to brace himself, to keep his knees from buckling. "Sam…"

Sam leaned forward, taking the head of Elijah's cock between her lips, and Logan's entire body went rock hard. It was wickedly sensual to see her suck Elijah into her mouth.

"Fuck," Elijah groaned again. He didn't make a move to touch her, probably because he didn't want the intensity to dissipate.

Logan knew quite extensively just how good it felt to have Sam's mouth wrapped around his cock, and Elijah was experiencing it for the very first time.

Based on the look on Elijah's face, this wasn't going to be the last time, either.

---

HER MOUTH WAS FUCKING HEAVEN. SWEET AND hot and… Elijah could hardly think for the sheer ethereal pleasure that accosted him.

He wanted to thrust his hips forward, to feel her wrapped around him completely, but he held back. He wanted her to touch him, to do what she wanted, to lead the way. He was quite content with just feeling.

It had been a long damn time since he'd done something like this. And it had nothing to do with a woman's mouth wrapped around his dick. Elijah wasn't a saint in any sense of the word. He'd been with plenty of women, but not since Beth had he felt an emotional pull to someone. Not like this.

Sam wasn't feasting on him; she wasn't trying to push him to the brink. She was taking her time, and that, above all else, was making him insane with need. A need so fierce he wondered how long tonight would last. If he had to guess, it wouldn't be long.

Because he didn't want to come, didn't want to put an end to what might just be the most amazing night he'd had in the last... God, it had been almost six years since Beth had gotten sick. Elijah gripped the base of his cock, tightening his fingers to keep himself from letting go too soon.

"Aww, Sam," he growled. "Baby, it's too good. I... Fuck, your mouth is sweet."

Sam moaned in response, but she didn't pull away. Thank Christ. He didn't want her to pull away, didn't want her to stop touching him.

But he knew she would have to, because he wanted to touch her, to feel her, to taste her. He wanted it with a passion that had long been dormant.

Unable to take any more, Elijah pulled out of her mouth and glanced up at Logan.

"Let's take this to the couch," Logan suggested, nodding toward an oversized outdoor sofa that looked to have been designed just for these instances.

Elijah offered Sam his hand, helping her to stand as Logan did. They each took one of her hands and led her over to the sofa. That's when Elijah looked to Logan once more. This was the point of no return, and he needed the other man to acknowledge it. Elijah wasn't here just for sex. He wasn't interested in Sam blowing him, or riding him until he came. That wasn't his main objective.

"Lie on the couch, Sam," Logan told her, his eyes still locked with Elijah's. "Tonight's all about you, baby."

The man definitely understood.

While Logan began to undress, Elijah helped Sam over to the couch, assisting her as she lay flat on her back. When she was in place, Elijah situated his knee between her thighs and climbed over her so that he was directly atop her, holding his weight with his arms.

"Sam," he whispered, his heart pounding loudly enough to be heard by the neighbors. "Kiss me, Samantha."

And with that, Elijah lowered his head and met her lips with his. Briefly. Tentatively. Just a soft caress of her mouth against his until she sighed. When she did, he slipped his tongue past her lips and into her mouth, meeting hers.

The world exploded behind his closed eyes; a light show of epic proportions went off as their tongues melded together, seeking, searching.

Oh, fuck. He hadn't kissed a woman like this ... in a long, long time.

Knowing Logan would be joining them, Elijah managed to move over to Sam's side, his back against the cushions of the couch, their mouths never separating.

Elijah opened his eyes to see Logan join them, his long, trim body laid out on Sam's other side. Elijah pulled her closer to him to offer the other man more room. With Sam on her back, sandwiched between them while they rested on their sides facing her, neither of them was hindered from taking what he sought.

Pulling his mouth from hers, Elijah continued to watch as Logan tipped her chin toward him and pressed his lips to hers. God, that was hot. Sam met Logan's lips with the same passion she'd met his with. The kiss lingered until it heated another notch, getting hotter, igniting into an inferno of need that was threatening to consume them all.

Elijah didn't wait to be invited. He shifted slightly and then leaned down to take the tip of Sam's perfect pink nipple into his mouth, teasing it with the tip of his tongue.

She moaned, the sound muffled by Logan's mouth on hers, but that only encouraged Elijah to continue. To drive her as crazy as she was driving him.

The next thing he knew, Sam's hand was in his hair, holding him to her, and Logan was torturing her other breast with his mouth while she cried out.

"God, yes. Please, touch me. Logan. Elijah. I need you both."

Elijah's body trembled from her words. She had said his name, and he was surprised he hadn't gone off right then and there.

When Elijah pulled back, Logan did also, and the two of them looked at one another over her naked body.

"Taste her," Logan instructed him before turning his attention to Sam. "Do you want Eli to lick your pussy, baby?"

"Yes, please," she begged, arching her back as though she were trying to get closer to them both.

"How bad do you want it?" Logan asked her. "Tell us."

"God, please, Elijah. Yes, lick me."

Elijah pressed his lips to her mouth one last time as he crawled over her once again, his knee between her thighs, the warmth of her pussy pressed against him. He released her lips and then kissed a trail down her sternum, between her breasts, over her stomach. Due to the proximity, his arm brushed against Logan's chest, but neither of them jerked away as though they'd been burned.

"Please," Sam pleaded again, louder this time. "I need you, Eli."

Oh, hell.

Elijah knew he was a goner. Right then and there.

# CHAPTER TWELVE

SAM WASN'T ABOVE BEGGING. IN FACT, SHE would've gotten down on her knees if she'd thought it would help, but that would defeat the purpose. Right now, she was right where she wanted to be.

These two men ... their hands on her. Their bodies crushed against hers, they filled her with warmth, with blinding, aching need. But more than that, they filled her with a sense of security that she usually only received from Logan.

"Lift your head, baby," Logan urged, briefly distracting her from the man kneeling between her thighs.

Sam lifted her head and felt the blindfold give. Logan was removing it. She kept her eyes closed briefly, peeking out until she could get used to the dim light that surrounded them. Once she did, she glanced down to see Elijah between her legs, his incredible body solid and tight, and his hair mussed from where she'd grabbed his head only moments before.

"I want you to watch him," Logan told her, still lying at her side.

Sam took Logan's hand, twining their fingers as she glanced up at him. She smiled, and when he smiled back, she knew he was just as caught up in the moment as she was.

"Oh, God!" Sam cried out as Elijah pressed his mouth to her pussy, his tongue sliding between her folds. There had been no warning, although if she'd been paying attention, she should've seen him lower his head.

"Does it feel good?" Logan asked.

"So good," she answered. "Please don't stop."

Pressing her hips up, she ground her pussy against Elijah's mouth, the harsh stubble on his chin and cheeks abrading the insides of her thighs, but she didn't care. The heat of his tongue was intoxicating. Her body tightened, the first of what she hoped were many orgasms cresting.

"Elijah!" Sam screamed his name as she came, unable to hold back. What had started out as a gentle ripple in her core radiated outward and crested, slamming through her with an intensity that sucked the air from her lungs. Just the sight of the beautiful man between her legs doing wicked things with his tongue had set her off.

"Don't stop," Logan told Elijah. "I want to watch her come again."

And Elijah followed Logan's directions without question. He continued to torment her, his tongue sliding against her clit, lashing at it, until she was nearly begging him to stop. She was overly sensitive from her first orgasm, and the man clearly knew it, but he didn't let up... And he didn't let up still.

"Oh, God!" Sam cried out, squeezing Logan's hand and reaching for Elijah's head, her fingers grasping his soft, silky hair.

"Come for us, baby," Logan said, his mouth hovering above hers. "It's fucking hot to watch him eat your pussy."

Oh, God. Logan's words were almost enough to push her over again.

Almost.

Elijah must've known she was close, because he thrust one finger into her, then another, and Sam was skyrocketing into another blissful orgasm.

Before she knew what was happening, Elijah was at her other side once more. This time he was pulling her to him, and she went without hesitation. He kissed her. Hard. Not a gentle, tender kiss like they'd shared earlier. This one was full of passion and hunger.

And need.

Oh, God, the man could kiss. This was a soul kiss, one that penetrated her entire body.

Sam felt Logan's body over hers, his chest against her back, sandwiching her between him and Elijah. He didn't put his full weight on her, but the heat from his naked chest was enough.

His head came close to theirs, and Sam pulled away from Elijah and kissed Logan. She found herself alternating between the two of them as she rocked between them, engulfed by their warmth, wanting to feel them inside of her.

Before she could beg, plead, or ask, Logan was moving, kneeling behind her as Elijah pulled her up his body. Once again, their mouths met, their tongues sliding together.

"Fuck," Elijah groaned, and Sam pulled back, staring down at him. He smiled and Sam's heart double-timed. "Sorry, that was ... a little unexpected."

Sam raised an eyebrow in question, unsure what he was referring to. "The condom," Elijah said, laughing.

Sam turned to see Logan opening a foil wrapper and retrieving the condom inside.

"I need to be inside of you, Sam. Right now." Elijah's tone was coarse, his words clipped. As though he was hanging on by sheer will.

Sam knew just how he felt. The anticipation was going to drive her insane.

Sam adjusted so that Elijah's cock was pressed against her, and that's when she realized he was already suited up. Which meant ... Logan had put the condom on Elijah.

That made her laugh. Clearly, her husband was in a hurry.

Without further ado, Elijah gripped his cock, and Sam eased him inside of her, holding her breath. He was big. Not quite as thick as Logan, but enough to stretch her completely.

"Oh, yes," she moaned, staring down at him. She was sitting up, her knees planted on each side of his narrow hips, her thighs straining to keep her from crashing into him, her hand gripping the back of the couch to keep her from falling over.

She lowered herself slowly, his cock brushing against nerve endings that were begging for more.

As soon as Elijah was deep inside of her, he pulled her back down so that she was resting against him once more.

"Tight," he growled. "So tight. Sam... Oh, God, Sam..."

Sam leaned down and kissed him. The man stole her breath with his words. Or more accurately, the emotion she felt behind them. The way he repeatedly said her name, as though grounding himself in the moment. Elijah wasn't just here for the sex, although, damn, it was well worth it.

No, the way he looked at her, touched her, spoke to her ... Sam knew it was far deeper than just physical gratification. She'd seen the same look in Logan's eyes just moments before.

Logan's hands gripped her hips, and Sam stopped rocking against Elijah. She pulled her lips from his and gazed down into Elijah's eyes for a brief moment. Turning, she glanced over her shoulder to see Logan staring back at her, his heart in his eyes.

"Logan." Sam met his gaze. "I need you."

He leaned forward, pressing his lips to her back. She had to turn back to face Elijah so that she didn't strain her neck, and when she did, Elijah gripped her thighs, pulling her to him so he went even deeper.

"Don't move," Logan warned them, his hand pressing down on Sam's back. "I'm going to fuck your sweet ass, baby."

His voice sounded tortured, and Sam knew he was hanging on by the same frayed thread that she was. It had been a long time since they'd done this. Her body craved it. Craved both of these men.

And she was tired of waiting.

LOGAN HAD EXPECTED TO BE JEALOUS. EVEN a little bit.

Oddly, he wasn't.

The emotion he felt was strange. Foreign. But it wasn't even remotely close to jealousy.

No, the fact that Elijah was there, his entire focus on Sam, looking at her as though she were the most important woman in the entire world... Well, it settled Logan somewhat. Elijah wouldn't hurt her. And Logan had a good feeling he wouldn't walk away from her, either.

That's what Sam needed.

What *he* needed.

Even if he hadn't realized it until tonight. But it was true.

Logan gripped his dick, squeezing it tightly to keep from coming right there on Sam's naked back. He had placed the condom on Elijah so they could get on with it. At first, the idea had weirded him out, but it was a hell of a lot easier than he'd thought. It was intimate, yet not. It did nothing for Logan to touch Elijah, but he had accomplished his goal, and now he could see Elijah buried to the hilt inside of Sam, her pussy stretched around him as she arched forward, her ass thrust high in the air.

Fuck.

Grabbing the tube of lubrication, Logan squeezed a generous amount on Sam's exposed hole before coating his condom-covered cock.

He had to place his hand on Sam's back once more, to get her to lower herself and provide him with a better angle. But then she was perfectly positioned and he was lining up, the head of his cock disappearing into her slowly.

Hot. So fucking hot. And tight.

He ground his teeth together as her body tightened and her back stiffened.

"Relax for me, Sam. Bear down, right now." When she did, Logan pushed in deeper, doing his best to go slow, only, fuck... That tight ring of muscles squeezed him, her body pulling him in.

"Oh, God. It..." Sam didn't get a chance to finish her sentence because Elijah had pulled her head down, their mouths crushed together.

Sweat was beading on Logan's forehead, his chest, his forearms, by the time he was fully seated inside of Sam, the firm ridge of Elijah's cock pressed against him inside of her.

Tight. So fucking tight.

"Damn," Elijah growled, his hips thrusting up, rocking Sam's body.

Logan closed his eyes, pulled out slowly, and then entered her again. He did this over and over, only now he was watching them. Watching where he and Elijah were filling her, the way Elijah held her hips and pressed up inside of her when Logan retreated. They'd established a rhythm that Sam seemed to enjoy, because she was moaning, her head tossed back.

"Does it feel good, Sam?" Elijah asked, his accent a little thicker than before. "Do you like to be filled by both of us?"

"Yes," she said, her voice strained.

"Your pussy's so tight," Elijah told her. "I bet your ass is strangling Logan."

"Fuck yes," Logan growled as he thrust back inside of her.

"Are you ready to come for us?" Elijah was the one doing all the talking now.

"Yes. Make me come, Elijah. Logan, please make me come."

Logan's heart swelled. The sound of his name on her lips did that to him, though.

Unable to refrain any longer, Logan began to thrust deeper, harder. Over and over, in time with Elijah's shallow thrusts from beneath her. It wasn't until Sam announced that she was coming at the same time she reached back and clawed Logan's thigh that he finally reached the pinnacle. That was what pushed Logan right over the edge, hard and fast.

"Fuck! I'm coming."

"Oh, yeah," Elijah said, his cock pulsing against Logan's deep inside of Sam. "Fuck yes."

# CHAPTER THIRTEEN

FRIDAY MORNING, ELIJAH FOUND HIMSELF ROAMING HIS small house, pacing the floors as his mind continued to replay the night he'd spent with Sam and Logan. A constant loop that didn't want to stop.

Three days had passed since Elijah had gone to their house. Three long days that he'd spent immersed in work. Another trip to Florida — hopefully the last — keeping his mind off of all of the emotions that had been plaguing him. His plane had been delayed last night, and he hadn't made it back to the house until midnight, which was why he hadn't bothered to go into the office that morning. At least not yet. He was working that direction, trying to get himself focused, but it wasn't working.

Even with work and all of the chaos that came along with it, he'd been unable to stop thinking about that night.

It had been incredible.

Beyond incredible.

But that was what sex was supposed to be like, right?

Sure. Didn't mean that it always was.

Not since Beth and James.

*Shit.*

Elijah dropped into one of the overstuffed chairs, running his hand through his hair.

The current erotic movie running through his head was superimposed with the memories of so many years ago. It had to have been close to six years ago, now that he thought about it.

Before Beth had gotten sick.

He and James, his best friend since college, had surprised her one night. She had called Elijah at work that morning to let him know she would be home early, so he had made a point to get home before her.

*"You made me dinner," Beth said when she came into the house just a little after four in the afternoon.*

*"We did," James told her, passing Elijah as he went to greet her appropriately.*

*"I'm not sure if I should be happy or scared," Beth told him when James pulled her to him, softly kissing her on the mouth.*

*"Scared," James mumbled. "You should be very, very scared. Because tonight, it's all about you. The things we're going to do to you..."*

That night they had been observing an anniversary of sorts. One that celebrated the very first time the three of them had been together. Had they really been together *that* long? Yes, they had. That night marked the third anniversary, although, at the time, it had felt like it had all begun not long ago.

Yeah, it wasn't long after that third anniversary that Beth had gotten sick and James ... well, James had had a meltdown.

*"I can't do it, Eli. Can't. It breaks my heart to watch her. I want to take away her pain, but there's nothing I can do to help her. She told me to go, told me to move on."*

*"She needs you, J. She needs us both," Elijah argued.*

*"She needs you, not me. She needs someone strong enough to help her through this. I'm not that man."*

*"Don't do this. Don't turn your back on her, goddammit!"*

*"I have to," James said, defeated.*

*"You're a bastard, you know that?" Elijah barked.*

*"I know,"* James answered, not an ounce of anger in his voice. *"I know."*

There was no doubt that James had fallen in love with Beth the same way that Elijah had. But according to Beth, she had never loved James that way, which was why she'd asked him to go before the worst of it had ever hit, before Beth was nothing more than a shell of her former self.

Elijah wasn't sure that was the case, not even now, but he knew Beth. She'd been trying to protect him *and* James. When she'd first found out about the cancer, it had been advanced. Far more advanced than they had expected. For the two years before she'd died, Beth had insisted that she live life to its fullest.

With Elijah. And only him.

James had fallen apart at the news that Beth had been sick, and shortly after their argument, he had disappeared from their lives. When Beth had died, Elijah had tried to find him, needing his best friend to lean on, someone who could understand the brutal loss that he was consumed by. But to no avail.

His heart hurt from the memories.

His beautiful Beth.

She'd been the love of his life. No woman would ever be able to take her place. No woman would ever reach that part of him that had been reserved solely for her.

That didn't mean that Samantha hadn't touched another part of him. One that was looking for her, hoping for what she could offer him, and it had nothing to do with sex and everything to do with that other part of him that needed to be needed.

Elijah's phone rang, pulling him from his thoughts. He pushed out of the chair and headed for the kitchen, where he'd left his phone.

Fully expecting it to be some major emergency that required him to get his ass into the office, Elijah snatched the phone up, hit the talk button without even looking at the screen.

"Hello," he greeted formally.

"Hey, man. How's it going?"

Logan. Not work.

"Good," Elijah said, hoping he didn't sound like he was lying.

"Hey, I know it's Friday and you're probably at work, but I wanted to see if you could get away early. We'll go out and catch a ball game tonight? I have box seats, and they're just going to go to waste if we don't use them. My brother and his husband are going with."

Elijah had turned down Logan's previous invitation to play golf because he'd had to leave town, but this time there wasn't anything that would get in his way. He definitely had enough vacation time to afford to take a few hours off on a Friday. Hell, he ought to take the whole day. His mind was that messed up.

As much as he wanted to sit in the dark and wallow in self-pity, he knew it wasn't the best way to pass the time.

"Yeah," he found himself saying. "That'd be great."

"I'll stop by and pick you up around five. Game starts at seven. Then we'll head over to Luke's and pick them up on the way."

"I'll be here."

The call ended and Elijah stood in the middle of his living room.

A ball game.

With Logan.

It felt almost like deja vu. Something he would've done with James all those years ago. Not only had they shared Beth, but he and James had been close. And now he had another chance at the friendship that had been stolen from him because James had been ... scared.


By seven o'clock, Elijah, Logan, Luke, and Cole were at Globe Life Park in Arlington watching the Texas Rangers take on the Boston Red Sox.

The game had started out slow, but the beer was cold, the crowd was enjoying themselves, and Elijah had finally relaxed. Luke and Cole had been bickering about something, keeping all of them laughing since the moment they'd gotten into the car.

But it was relatively quiet at the moment because Luke and Cole had headed off to get more beer rather than wait for someone to deliver it to them. It smelled like a setup, but Elijah didn't say anything.

"Tell me about James," Logan suggested, glancing over at him. The man was leaning forward, his elbows resting on his knees as he watched the game.

Yep, definitely a setup.

Elijah contemplated what he should tell Logan briefly. During the drive to get Luke and Cole, they had talked but mostly about work, about Elijah's trips, and how often he was out of town or out of the country. As it turned out, they both travelled, although Logan didn't leave town nearly as often, and when he did, it was usually for a day or two at most. Elijah had reluctantly informed Logan that he was generally gone for at least fifteen out of every thirty.

The discussion had been relatively casual, but Elijah had heard Logan's interest, and in turn, he'd been curious himself. So, he opted to go for open and honest.

"I met James in college. We started off as roommates and became good friends. After we graduated, James bought a house and I rented a room from him. I had started out at VI as a sales rep making little to nothing at first, but I quickly started climbing the ladder."

"So it's always been sales for you?"

"It has. I'm good at it, for whatever reason. VI had me going to trade shows, said I had charisma. I don't know about all that, but I was good with people."

"Was?" Logan asked, grinning.

"Okay. Am. I *am* good with people. That's when I met Beth. I somehow, by the grace of God, managed to catch her eye, and by the time I had the nerve to ask her out that same day, she admitted she'd been hoping I would.

"Anyway, I'd known Beth for only a few months before I introduced her to James. I think James fell in love with her right away although we were all just friends. But they became close. Beth and I bought a house, I moved out of James', but we still saw him all the time. After we were married, he'd stay at the house, and the three of us hung out almost every day."

Logan glanced over at him briefly before turning back to watch the action.

Elijah continued, "James was my best man at my wedding. He was going to be the godfather of our children if we ever had them."

"Did you want children?" Logan asked.

"Beth did. I was on the fence. When she got sick, it no longer mattered, although she kept telling me she wished we'd had a baby so I wouldn't be alone."

"Would it've helped?" Logan sat back in his seat, crossing one ankle over the opposite knee as he regarded him.

"No," Elijah told him point-blank. "Nothing would've eased the pain of losing her." Elijah watched the game for a moment, waited until the man at bat struck out before turning his attention back to Logan. "What about you? Do you and Sam plan to have kids?"

"No," Logan answered quickly, a small smile. "We both know we're not cut out for it. Hell, I had a dog — Bear, who is now my brother's dog — and I couldn't keep him. When work is your main priority, it's challenging to take care of someone else."

"You and Sam are a match then, huh? She's just as focused as you are."

Logan laughed roughly. "From what I've seen, *you* make the two of us look like slackers."

Elijah laughed, too, but it faded quickly. "I didn't work this much after I met Beth. And definitely not after we were engaged. She was my life. Work was secondary."

"I know how that feels," Logan said, and this time it was his turn to glance out over the ballpark. "If it weren't for the fact I see Sam every day at the office, I'd spend a lot less time there."

Right then, Luke and Cole returned, handing off two beers, one to Elijah, the other to Logan, before they dropped into their seats behind Logan.

For a few minutes, no one spoke, aside from making a comment about the game. At least until Luke decided to throw out the question of the hour.

---

"So, WHAT ARE YOUR INTENTIONS WITH MY boy here?"

*Boy?* Logan fought the urge to laugh at his brother, but he did roll his eyes. He'd fully expected Luke to put in his two cents, to give Elijah a tough time. That's what Luke did. He didn't want to open up about himself, but he didn't have any qualms about calling others to the carpet.

Elijah glanced behind Logan at Luke, a smile on his face.

"If you're asking if I plan to marry him, sorry to let you down, but that's not on my agenda."

"What *is* on your agenda?" Luke asked, his voice lowered, his tone serious.

Elijah glanced at Logan and he merely shrugged. If Elijah wanted to blow Luke off, he couldn't blame the guy. What they did wasn't any of Luke's business.

"I was planning to sit here with my beer, enjoy the game. What's on *your* agenda?" Elijah retorted, still keeping a measure of humor in his eyes although Logan felt his tension.

"Are you serious about this?" Luke asked bluntly.

"*This?* Is that how you see it?" Elijah said, lowering his voice a notch. "Why don't you call it what it is? A relationship. Something more than friendship, maybe? And if, by 'this,' you're referring to Samantha, at least have the decency to address her as a person."

"*This,*" Luke repeated. "This relationship. I take it you're not interested in my brother, because unlike me, he doesn't swing both ways."

Elijah's brows furrowed slightly as he stared back at Luke over his shoulder. "I don't swing both ways, either. Not that there's anything wrong with that."

Logan was pretty sure he heard Luke sigh in relief, probably glad to hear Elijah didn't have a problem with his relationship with Cole.

It had taken a lot to get Luke to come to terms with the fact that he loved Sierra *and* Cole. Not only did he have a problem with the 'and' part of that statement, he had a major issue with the fact that he was attracted to Cole. But they'd finally come around, and life had looked up for his brother. For that, Logan was grateful.

But in the same sense, Logan wasn't looking for the same thing Luke had found. He could absolutely see himself becoming friends with Elijah. Hell, they already were. Not only did Logan look forward to seeing Elijah with Sam, he also looked forward to seeing Elijah period. Strange, that.

There might not be a sexual connection between him and Elijah, but Logan had the overwhelming urge to shield Elijah. To help him through this. The man was clearly still hurting, keeping himself locked away, and Logan could relate. He hadn't lost Sam, and he prayed he never had to go through that, but Logan had lost his parents. He'd been young, and the pain of their death still echoed inside of him.

That sort of loss would never go away.

But it did eventually get easier to breathe. And Logan knew that when Elijah was around Sam, he was breathing a little easier.

"Lay off, man," Logan finally told Luke. "We've got it covered. But I promise, when we need relationship advice, you'll be the first person we come to."

That made Cole laugh uncontrollably, which eased the tension. Luke turned his feigned wrath on his lover, and that got the two of them squabbling again.

Yep, overall, life was good.

# CHAPTER FOURTEEN

ELIJAH WAS WANDERING THE HOUSE THE FOLLOWING morning, still exhausted from the night before. He'd slept in later than usual, but that hadn't helped all that much even though, for the first time in a long time, Elijah hadn't dreamed. About anything.

At least not that he could remember.

He and Logan had had a good time at the game, even stopped off to have wings for dinner after they'd dropped Luke and Cole back at their house. By the time that was all said and done, Logan had dropped him off close to one in the morning.

It had been a long time since Elijah had been out with friends like that. Usually it was business associates, and with those relationships, he always ensured he kept them at a distance. Not to mention, most people he worked with tiptoed around the subjects they believed would send Elijah into an emotional tailspin.

Not Logan. He was up-front, curious, and he didn't have a problem asking the difficult questions. At one point, they'd even talked about Logan's parents. Apparently, they'd died in a car accident — killed by a drunk driver when he and Luke were eight. To an eight-year-old, his life had been irrevocably damaged. According to Logan, his grandfather had stepped in and raised them.

The man had done a damn fine job as far as Elijah was concerned.

Elijah had seen a different side of Logan last night. It was clear to him that the man was making a point to get to know him and to share a bit of himself along the way. Something he doubted Logan did with everyone.

Now that he was awake, the empty house providing only deafening silence, Elijah suddenly missed the company. Even Luke and his prodding ways. Logan's twin was a pain in the ass, but Elijah found he respected the guy. Cole had playfully informed him yesterday that Luke wasn't *trying* to be an ass. He was just naturally an ass.

But Elijah had held his own with Luke. He fully intended to see where this went with Logan and Sam, and he wasn't at all bothered by Logan's brother being overbearing and overprotective.

Elijah was just making his way into the kitchen to make coffee when his cell phone rang. He retrieved the phone from the bar, where he'd placed it when he'd fumbled through the house in the middle of the night. The screen lit up with Logan's number and he answered.

"You can't say you left something in my car last night. That won't work since we went in yours."

Logan laughed.

"What's up?" Elijah asked as he continued toward the kitchen, phone to his ear. He needed coffee before he could handle any conversation, lengthy or otherwise.

"I have a favor to ask."

Elijah wasn't sure he liked the sound of that.

"I've got to head out of town. I just got an emergency call from Xavier, although you can bet your ass it isn't as dire as the man made it sound. But, nonetheless, I've got to go take care of this for him. I was planning to take Sam to the art gallery tonight. There's an exhibit she's been wanting to see."

"I'll take her," Elijah said, cutting Logan off. The man didn't have to convince him. "I'd be honored to take her," he clarified.

"I'd say thank you, but I don't think it's necessary," Logan said, clearly catching on to Elijah's intentions.

"No, it's not. In fact, I think you're doing *me* a favor."

Logan was silent for a moment, except for the sound of movement on the other end. "Hey, I meant to tell you this yesterday … about the other night … you didn't have to leave. I want you to know that."

Yeah, he did, but he wasn't about to tell Logan that. That night had been more than Elijah had originally bargained for, but no less than what he'd expected after he'd met Samantha. Tonight, seeing Samantha again, he feared, would probably solidify what he was already suspecting. "I'll remember that next time."

"Look, Eli," Logan began, "I don't know what your experience is in these situations, but…"

"But what?" Elijah encouraged.

"Sam hasn't been in a lot of these situations, but I can tell you that what happened that night … that was a first for us. And yes, for both of us. I've never wanted to share her. Not … like that."

Elijah stopped working on the coffee and turned to lean against the counter. He was a little shaken by the direction Logan had taken the conversation. He was also grateful the man hadn't opted to talk about it yesterday. Face-to-face. That would've been … awkward.

"The feeling's mutual," Elijah offered truthfully. "It was … intense."

"Good word for it," Logan agreed. "I don't see this being something that is going to go slow. I don't expect it to, either. And about tonight, I'd really like for you and Sam to see where this goes. I'll be back tomorrow afternoon sometime, so... Fuck."

Elijah could hear the frustration in Logan's tone. So, clearly this wasn't easy for either of them.

"Take care of her for me. I think you already know that she deserves that and so much more."

"So much more," Elijah echoed. More than Elijah could probably give her. But surprisingly, he was willing to try. He hadn't felt this way about anyone in four long, painful years, and now that he remembered what it felt like, he wasn't ready to let it go. "I'll take care of her, Logan."

"Thanks. Look, I've got to run. The gallery opens at six, I think. I haven't said anything to Sam. I figured you'd want to have the honor of asking her."

"Thanks," Elijah said, at a loss for words.

The call ended, and Elijah stood there, staring at the blank screen on his phone for the longest time.

Logan had just handed Samantha to him on a silver platter. What he chose to do with the offer could very well alter the course of their lives.

Elijah hit the button to bring the screen on his phone back to life.

Now, it was time to take the first step.

---

"HEY, BABY," LOGAN CALLED TO SAM HALF an hour later. He'd heard her cell phone ring, knew who it was on the other end, so he had left her alone when she'd wandered back to their bedroom, phone to her ear. She had just hung up and was walking back toward the kitchen, where he was sitting at the table, his laptop open in front of him.

"That was Elijah," she explained. "He asked if he could take me to the art exhibit tonight. You work fast, don't you?" she asked with a huge grin.

"What? I just called him to let him know I had to go out of town. It was up to him to do with that information as he saw fit. For him to call you was his decision, not mine."

Sam walked up to him, and Logan leaned back in his chair.

As she did frequently, she straddled his lap, placing her hands on his shoulders. "Now is the time I feel like I'm supposed to ask you if you're all right with this," Sam said, placing her finger over his lips when he started to respond. "But I don't think I have to ask that. I can tell. Something is ... different. About this whole situation. I don't know what it is, but I feel it."

"I feel it, too," Logan told her.

"This isn't just sex. Is it?"

"No," he said straightforwardly.

It wasn't for him. Then again, sex with Samantha had never been "just sex" for him. He'd known it from the moment he'd seen her that this woman owned him. Heart and soul.

And to top it off, she accepted his idiosyncrasies. She craved them as much as he did. And polyamory was unquestionably one of them that they both wanted. Although before Elijah, Logan would've said he was only interested in the sex part.

As his relationship with Sam continued to grow and strengthen, Logan realized that what they wanted was more. More than just sex, as she'd put it.

"I'm going on a date with Elijah tonight," she told him, although he already knew that.

"And?"

"And ... what if he invites me back to his place?"

"Do you want to go back to his place?"

"Maybe... Probably. Does that seem like I'm cheating on you?"

"No," he told her adamantly, looking directly into her eyes. "Sam, you've known this was something we both wanted from the beginning. I introduced you to this lifestyle, and neither of us questioned it then, so why are you questioning it now?"

"Luke wasn't serious about me, and I wasn't serious about him. Nor was Tag. They were... God, I hate to say it, but they were casual. We knew it was just for the sex."

"No, *I* knew it," Logan corrected. "I wasn't willing to share all of you with them."

"But you're willing to share all of me with Elijah? Why?"

"Fuck if I know," he told her truthfully. "I don't question my gut feelings, Sam. From the moment I met him, I knew that what he represented was more than just casual. This is a lifestyle for him. Or at least it was when his wife was alive. I don't think he's been serious about anyone in a long time."

"He's serious about this," Sam told him. "He and I just hashed this out over the phone. I figured we'd lay all of our cards on the table up front. It's what the three of us deserve."

"I agree." Logan was glad that they had. He'd expected it. As much as he had expected to have this discussion with Sam. The two of them. This new situation was going to change their lives in ways they'd probably never expected.

But in a sense, Logan *had* expected it.

And he found that he wanted it. For whatever reason, he wanted to share Sam with Elijah. And maybe he had only been willing to share her body for a while. Or maybe he'd always wanted something more. That was why he'd invited Tag, believing the man was close enough to them that he wouldn't hurt Sam. But he had. Inadvertently, sure. But he'd hurt her all the same.

Logan didn't want anyone to hurt Sam.

"I don't want casual any more than you do," he explained. "If I'm going to share you—"

"God, do we have to use that word? Share? You're not sharing me," she told him abruptly. "I don't see it that way. I don't feel as though I don't belong to you. When you say share, it's as though you feel like I'm something you could toss away. This is something that you and I choose to do together."

Logan felt his heart constrict. He loved this woman. Beyond words.

"I'm going to go to the art exhibit with Elijah tonight. If he invites me back to his place, I'll probably say yes."

"What if you invite him back here?" Logan asked, his eyes watching her.

"I was wondering the same thing," she whispered. "I would prefer that we were here. That way, should you come home, we'd be here for you. I don't want to be anywhere else, Logan."

"Then bring him here."

"We've never..."

Logan knew where she was going. They had shared plenty of threesomes at their house. In the shower, in the pool, on the back porch, the hot tub, the kitchen table. Anywhere but their bedroom. Their bed.

But ... that's what she was hinting at.

A hot poker of lust scorched him from the inside just thinking about walking in to find Sam in bed with Elijah, the two of them...

"You're thinking about it," Sam said, a smile on her lips. "You're thinking about walking in on us, aren't you? Would you like that?"

"Fuck yeah," he groaned. "Walking in to find you riding him, your hair falling down your back, your breasts" — Logan cupped her breasts as he spoke — "swaying above his face. Fuck yeah, that's hot."

"Would you join us? Or would you watch?"

"I'd watch at first. Watch what he does to you, watch how he makes you come. Then I'd join you."

Sam scooted forward, the heat between her thighs rubbing along his cock. The only thing separating them was a pair of loose cotton shorts that he had on and the panties that she wore. She'd come out of the bedroom wearing one of his dress shirts, which came down to her knees.

Logan unbuttoned one of the buttons on her shirt with his teeth, pushing the fabric aside to reveal her naked breast. "Fuck, you're hot. I bet you're wet just thinking about it, aren't you?"

"Yes," she whispered, her fingers threading into his hair and pulling him close. He latched on to her nipple with his lips, using his teeth to nibble until she was grinding against him.

"You know I'm just going to tease you, don't you?" he asked when he pulled away.

"I figured as much. And I'm going to call you tonight and tell you how my date went."

Fuck. "Deal."

With that, Logan set forth to tease her more, but he never did let her come. Not even once.

# CHAPTER FIFTEEN

ELIJAH ARRIVED VIA LIMOUSINE TO PICK SAM up at five thirty. He was dressed just as magnificently as he had been every other time she'd seen him. His dark gray suit was tailored and expensive, his white shirt bright, and his red tie was eye-catching. The man had it going on.

She couldn't say that she was surprised. First, she knew Elijah was punctual; second, she knew he would go all out.

He hadn't come inside the house, either, merely complimenting her on how incredible she looked in her short, red dress — the fact that it matched his tie was not lost on her, either. She had worn this dress specifically for tonight. It was classy, sexy, and she knew Logan loved when she wore it, so she had hoped Elijah would like it, also.

But aside from being a total gentleman, Elijah had been surprisingly quiet during the drive from her house.

As the limo approached the art gallery, Sam accepted the silence. Elijah hadn't said more than ten words since they'd climbed inside. She couldn't tell if something was bothering him or not, and she figured, based on what she did know about him, he wasn't nervous, so she assumed something was on his mind.

When the back door opened, Elijah climbed out of the limo, holding his hand out to her so she could join him. Once she was on her feet, she situated her hand in the crook of his arm and allowed him to lead her inside.

Even in her heels, Elijah was taller than she was. He wasn't even remotely as tall as Logan was, but not many men were. He was, however, probably close to six feet. Maybe just under. But even in her heels, he was still a couple of inches taller. She liked that.

Oh, and she liked that the man smelled delicious.

The door to the gallery was opened by a well-dressed man with a bright white smile. Elijah nodded at him as they made their way inside.

Sam had been to this particular gallery before, but not this specific exhibit. She'd been asking Logan to take her for some time, but she knew it wasn't really his thing. He had intended to take her, though. He had promised. Unfortunately, business had come up, which, with either of them, that was to be expected from time to time.

A waiter moved toward them, carrying a tray of champagne flutes. Elijah retrieved two, handed one to her before they began their journey deeper into the gallery.

"I take it you enjoy art," Elijah prompted.

"I do. I went to my first art exhibit when I was in college. I don't go to many because I just don't make the time, but I have attended a few over the years. They're a fantastic distraction," she told him.

"I've attended a few myself."

"So there was no arm-twisting involved to get you to accompany me?" Sam asked lightheartedly.

"None whatsoever. In fact," Elijah said, turning to face her more directly, "it's my pleasure. One I hadn't quite expected."

The way that he was looking at her made her knees weak. His eyes were searching her face slowly before they landed on her mouth, and Sam couldn't hide her reaction from him.

After what had happened between the three of them almost a week ago, Sam had honestly been anxious to spend more time with Elijah, and it didn't even have to be horizontal time, either. In fact, she'd hoped for a little personal time. Time for them to talk. Like now.

She hadn't anticipated a one-on-one encounter, but she certainly wasn't disappointed. After all, she had given Logan a hard time about how he'd gotten to go out on a date with Elijah but she hadn't. Logan had punished her thoroughly for accusing him of dating a man, and that had been worth doing again. Logan's sensual brand of punishment was right up her alley.

It was a tad awkward because she did wish Logan were there, but she had set out to enjoy tonight.

She considered it an experience.

One she hoped wouldn't end abruptly, or with anyone getting hurt.

They fell into step once again, and as Sam took in an intricate sculpture on display, she opted to prompt Elijah to open up a little. What better opportunity than tonight, when they wouldn't be interrupted by anyone?

"Tell me about Beth," she urged, hoping he wouldn't pull away from her.

He didn't.

"Beth is the love of my life."

Sam noticed that he always referred to her in present tense.

"You met her through your work; you told me that," Sam said encouragingly. She wanted to know more about the woman who had stolen Elijah's heart. "What was she like?"

Elijah smiled and his entire face lit up. "She used to wake me up on Saturday morning so we could work in the yard. She loved to garden. It wasn't necessarily my thing," he said, glancing over at her, "but I did it because it put a smile on her face. You know those home and garden shows? She loved to go to them. We didn't usually leave with a single thing, or even an appointment, but she loved going."

"I don't think I could get Logan to go to a home and garden show if I begged," Sam said with a chuckle. They stopped in front of a small sculpture that required a little effort to make out what it was.

"And Beth loved movies. Any movie, she didn't care. At Christmas, she would insist that we watch all of the classics. Every year."

"What about you? Do you like movies?"

"Yes," Elijah said softly. "I guess I do. I enjoy concerts more. And I'm not talking about the opera, either."

"So, you're into music?"

"Yes. I'm a huge Eagles fan."

"Logan loves the Eagles, too," Sam told him. "We went to a concert in Vegas just a couple of years ago. I don't think his smile faded once the entire trip."

"And you? What do you enjoy doing? Besides attending art shows."

"Aside from work," Sam said, "I don't have much of a preference. I'm spontaneous, I guess you could say. I enjoy going to the clubs, even if it is just to socialize. I also enjoy movies, music, and yes, I've been known to enjoy an opera or two."

"Do you even realize how beautiful you are?" Elijah asked, staring back at her, his golden eyes sparkling.

"I do when Logan looks at me," she admitted, a little stunned by the abrupt change of the subject. "And you."

Elijah leaned in and kissed her. It was a soft, gentle press of his lips to hers, and it made her insides tingle and her heart do a strange flip in her chest. When he pulled back, she just stared up at him.

"I want to know everything there is to know about you, Sam."

"Ditto." Sam smiled. And it was the truth.

She wanted to know everything.

And then some.

ELIJAH HADN'T EXPECTED TO ENJOY THE ART gallery. And he'd been hesitant about taking Sam out without Logan, for whatever reason. But now that they were there, his reservations had dissipated, and the only thing he cared about was talking to the most beautiful woman in the room, the feel of her hand on his arm, the way her eyes sparkled when she laughed. It was more than he'd anticipated.

Even after the fireworks they'd created when the three of them had been together.

This was more. So much more.

They'd made their way through most of the gallery, stopping at all of the pieces that Sam seemed interested in, and their conversation had continued. Elijah had been surprised by how interested Sam was in him as a person. It had been a long time since a woman had reacted to him that way. Or maybe he just hadn't noticed it because, until Sam, he'd kept himself closed off to women.

A waiter passed, and Elijah handed him their empty glasses before taking Sam's hand in his. They continued to peruse the art that graced the walls and the various structures erected in the corners.

"So, tell me this... You said you had never had a threesome before you met Logan, correct?"

"That's right."

Sam didn't seem bothered by the subject, so Elijah continued.

"Your first time ... what was your reaction?"

"I think I was so overwhelmed, I didn't know what to think. It was similar to our first night. Only Logan kept the blindfold on me the entire time. I didn't even know what was going on until I realized there were more than two hands on me at one time. It wasn't until later that I saw Luke face-to-face. I had no clue Logan had a twin."

Elijah stopped. "You were in a threesome with Luke McCoy?"

"Yes," she said simply. "Long before Sierra came into the picture. Although Luke did have a thing for Cole at that point, but he was in denial about that, too. It didn't last long."

Sam's gaze left his as she glanced around the room.

"There was another time?" Elijah implored.

"Yes. I was introduced to Tag Murphy, and things ignited rather quickly; however, that fizzled out even faster than it had with Luke." Sam started walking again and Elijah remained at her side. "Once that was over, I realized I wasn't cut out for those emotional roller coasters. I love Logan. He owns my heart and soul. That will never change, but we both enjoy this ... other activity. Only I don't do casual sex well at all."

"And Logan didn't want to share all of you?" Based on how possessive Logan was about Sam, Elijah had thought he'd had a good understanding of what Logan did and didn't want from this, but his recent interactions with Logan had caused him to doubt his original belief.

"We don't see it as sharing me," she told him truthfully. "That sounds as though he doesn't love me. I know he does. I've never doubted his love for me. This is something we both want. We're experiencing it together."

"But you want more than just sex."

"Logan does, too," Sam said defensively. "He didn't expect more from Luke or Tag. They weren't the forever type, if you know what I mean. At least not for me."

Elijah stopped Sam when she started to walk away. "But I am?"

"I don't know," she whispered, her gaze colliding with his. "I just know that I feel something for you. There's a connection I'm not familiar with. At least not with anyone other than Logan. But I feel it with you."

"Does that bother you?"

"No," she said quickly.

"Does it bother Logan?"

"No. I asked him this morning. After you called. We don't assume to know what you're looking for, Eli, but I can tell you, this isn't casual. Not for either one of us. It's taken me a little by surprise, to be honest, but I take things one day at a time. At least now I do. Logan flipped my world upside down when I met him. I was confused, even scared about what I wanted when I was with him. But I've stopped fighting that part of myself. I don't care what other people think about me or my lifestyle. I just know what I want. What Logan wants."

Elijah took a step closer and placed his hands on Sam's hips. "I want to take you home," he said softly. "I want to explore your body with my hands, my lips, my tongue. I want to make love to you all night long, Samantha. I don't ever want to stop." Elijah paused, waited for her to argue. When she didn't, he continued. "But Logan isn't here, so I'm not expecting anything whatsoever. I can wait. As long as I have to. I've done this before. I understand the concept. I will never expect all of you, but I want more of you. I do know that much."

Sam's light green eyes glittered. What caused it, Elijah didn't know. What he did know was that she wanted this as much as he did.

"Take me home, Elijah," Sam whispered as her eyes dropped to his mouth and then back up again. "Take me home and stay the night with me. That's what I want right now."

Elijah took one step back. "I'll be glad to do just that," he told her, "but I need to call Logan first."

"I talked to Logan earlier today."

"I understand that. But you're his wife. I owe him the respect of calling him. Making sure he's all right with this. And then, once I've told him my intentions, we'll take it from there."

Sam nodded and Elijah didn't waste any time. He grabbed his cell phone and excused himself for a moment.

He didn't necessarily mind Sam overhearing, but Elijah did want a little privacy. For the most important phone call he feared he would ever make.

# CHAPTER SIXTEEN

BY THE TIME THE LIMO DROPPED THEM off at her house, Sam's nerves were staging a protest.

Elijah had talked to Logan briefly before they'd left the gallery. As had she. He'd given them their blessing, whispered a few naughty things into Sam's ear, and now that she and Elijah were walking into the dimly lit house, Sam felt like this was her first time ever being with a man.

How she had managed to keep her hands off Elijah in the limo was beyond her. She'd wanted to crawl into his lap and devour him whole. It would've been absolutely perfect if Logan had been there.

But he hadn't.

And this was new for her.

Despite the fact that she had Logan's approval, and she knew her husband would go wild when she gave him the play-by-play later, this still felt oddly like a date. As though Logan played no part in it whatsoever.

And that's what had her all mixed up inside.

"Would you like a drink?" she called to Elijah as she quickly made her way through the house, making a beeline for the kitchen.

"Sure," he said, his voice warm and sexy. "I'll have what you're having."

"Logan's got some scotch. You know, in case you prefer something other than fruity vodka." Sam did her best to lighten the mood, but it wasn't helping. Much. "But I'm sure we've got some whiskey or..."

When she reached the cabinet where they kept the liquor, Sam paused with her hand on the door handle. She took a deep breath. Let it out.

"Samantha." Elijah's voice came from right behind her.

Sam released her grip on the handle and turned to face him.

"Come here."

He didn't move closer, but she only had to take two steps before she was practically up against him.

Without another word, Elijah's big, warm hands cupped her face as he pressed his lips to hers. The kiss started slow, but it didn't take long before they were crushed together, her hands twisted in the lapels of his jacket, trying to get closer.

"I don't need anything to drink. I just need you. I want to make love to you, Sam."

Sam was breathless from his kiss, ready for more. If he'd expected her to argue, well, he had another thing coming. "I want the same thing."

"Do you have a guest bedroom?" Elijah asked.

It took Sam a moment to make out his question, but when she did, she just stood there, her mouth partially open.

"I won't make love to you in your bed, Sam. That's for you and Logan. I'll never cross that line. Do you have a guest bedroom?"

This time Sam nodded her head.

"Show me."

Sam was glad he could still talk, because her mouth had gone completely dry.

Elijah linked their fingers together, and Sam stared down at them briefly before meeting his gaze again.

Putting one foot in front of the other, Sam led him to the guest bedroom on the other side of the house.

Once inside, Elijah flipped on the switch, which happened to turn on the small lamp on the nightstand. The bed was highlighted by the soft, golden glow, the rest of the room kept in shadows. It was oddly romantic in an *I'm-taking-this-man-to-bed-in-our-guest-bedroom* sort of way.

"I like this room," she told him. "It was decorated long before I came along, but I love the colors. I don't think even before we were married that this room has ever actually had a guest stay in it." She was rambling but she couldn't help herself.

Elijah pressed up against her, his hands cupping her face again as he stared down at her. She loved when he did that. It made her feel cherished. As Elijah stood there, both of them transfixed on the other, he didn't say anything, but nothing really needed to be said. His eyes said it all. This was where they both wanted to be.

Pushing up on her toes, Samantha closed the gap between them, pressing her mouth to his. Sliding her hands up his chest, she linked them around his neck, teasing the hair at his nape. It was as soft as it looked.

"Sam," Elijah whispered before he thrust his tongue into her mouth, kissing her with so much passion she was convinced they might just burst into flames.

The next thing Sam knew, they were on the bed, both of them still dressed, except for her shoes, which she'd lost somewhere along the way.

Elijah was leaning over her, his finger trailing down her cheek as he stared back at her. His eyes penetrated her, as though he were asking that silent question. The one they seemed to have answered a million times, but due to the uncertainty, it continued to be asked.

Well, she wasn't going to let him ask it again. She knew what she wanted. She knew what he wanted. And right here, with Elijah, was where she wanted to be.

"Make love to me," she said breathlessly. "Make love to me, Eli."

To help him out, Sam lifted her head and reached behind her neck, untying the halter-top that would free her breasts. Thanks to the fancy construction of the dress, Sam had gone without a bra tonight, too. Once the fabric fell free, Elijah took over from there, sliding the silky material out of the way.

His warm palm cupped her breast lovingly, and Sam's breath stuttered in her chest again. When he leaned forward, teasing one nipple with the tip of his tongue, Sam watched him. God, that was hot. It wasn't long before she couldn't watch because she couldn't keep her eyes open.

The sensations were overwhelming, and she had to close her eyes as she thrust her chest forward, wanting more, needing all of him.

Elijah's hands joined in, and her dress slowly inched down her body until she was left in only her panties. She could feel Elijah's eyes as they trailed over her almost like a physical caress, one that made her skin tingle and her nipples harden even more.

She'd felt the penetrating heat of his eyes on her before. Strangely enough, it had been the night when she'd been blindfolded out by the pool. Even unable to see him, she'd felt him. His presence was that powerful.

"You are so beautiful, Samantha."

Sam wanted to hurry him along, to suggest he get naked so she could study him just as reverently, but it was apparent that Elijah was taking his time.

That was something they would have to work on.

---

TWO WEEKS AGO, ELIJAH WOULDN'T HAVE DREAMED that he'd be right here, hovering on the brink before this beautiful, married woman. But here he was, and the way his chest had swelled from the moment he'd laid eyes on Samantha again tonight, he knew he wouldn't want it any other way.

He'd been so overcome with emotions upon seeing her again that he'd been at a loss for words on the way to the gallery. He hadn't been able to express what he was feeling, so he'd just kept his mouth shut.

But then she'd asked him questions, and he'd found himself opening up to her.

After talking to Logan, ensuring the man didn't have a problem with his wife being with another man tonight, because yes, Elijah had given him the brunt of his intentions right away, Elijah had felt himself relax.

Sam, however, had not.

He could only imagine what this was like for her. He knew just how much she loved Logan, how much she wished he were there. And Elijah did, as well. Sort of.

Yet he knew he couldn't take tonight for granted, because despite this opportunity, he wasn't sure he'd get many chances to be alone with her. And yes, he wanted some alone time. That was the selfish part of him that needed to be needed.

His relationship with Beth and James had been similar. Beth had given James the time he'd needed, but she'd spent every night in Elijah's bed. Their bed. And it wasn't awkward. At least not for him.

Now he was on the other side looking in, and he wasn't bothered by it. Being this intimate, this emotionally attached to a woman who wasn't Beth had never factored into the equation, but here he was. Elijah wanted Sam. He wanted her to the depths of his soul. Tonight. Tomorrow night. And many, many nights to follow.

He was partly scared that he'd wake up and this would be a dream. Just like the many nights he dreamed of Beth, talking to her, laughing with her, holding her, kissing her... It all seemed so real, and then he'd wake up to a cold, lonely house.

But not tomorrow morning. Tomorrow he would wake up in this woman's arms. And he'd finally be warm again.

At least while she was with him.

Elijah pushed off of the bed, keeping his gaze fixed on Sam while he removed his clothes. He loved the way she looked at him, the way her eyes glazed as they lingered on every part of him that he uncovered.

Once he was naked, Elijah reached for Sam, pulling her panties down her long, smooth legs and tossing them into the pile with his clothes. Before he joined her on the bed, he reached for his wallet, which he'd placed on the night table.

Before he had the condom out and open, Sam was sitting up, her legs dangling over the side of the bed, on each side of his. She was smiling up at him, and her eyes flickered with what looked like mischief.

She was beautiful.

When Sam reached for him, her smooth fingers encircling his engorged cock, Elijah sucked in a breath. Fearful he'd drop it, Elijah tossed the condom onto the bed so they could get to it later. For now, she was touching him, and that was all that mattered.

Sliding his hands into her hair, he twined the long, gold strands around his fingers as she leaned forward and sucked him into her mouth.

"God, Sam," he groaned.

Elijah watched his dick slide past Sam's pretty pink lips, her tongue tormenting the sensitive underside of his cock as she laved him repeatedly.

It was too much.

He was on the brink of exploding. Just the sight of Sam had made him rock hard, and he'd battled his own need for her for so many hours that now he could barely control himself. And he damn sure didn't want to be in her mouth when he came. Not this time.

Easing her back by tugging her hair, he tilted her head so their eyes met. Planting one knee on the bed between her legs, he moved closer. Sam took the hint, scooting back on the bed until he could crawl on top of her. She fumbled for something, and Elijah realized she was searching for the condom he'd tossed there.

Smiling, he reached over and slipped the foil packet into her hand. Sam took over from there, opening the condom and then sheathing him quickly before she grabbed his ass and pulled him forward. Losing his balance, he tumbled on top of her. And when she laughed, his heart expanded at least two sizes.

"God, Sam," Elijah whispered, his finger trailing down her cheek. "Whatever am I going to do with you?"

"Make love to me?" she asked, her tone light. "Right now. Right here."

Holding his weight with one hand and one knee, Elijah reached between them and gripped his cock, lining himself up with her wet, hot entrance. He took a moment to tease her with his fingers, first her clit, then he slid one finger inside of her. When her eyes closed and a contented moan escaped, he pulled his hand back and slid home.

"Sam," he growled, the heat of her body clenching him tightly, holding him to her. "Oh, fuck, Sam."

Sam cupped his face the way he had hers earlier, and she kept her eyes pinned to his. "You feel so good, Eli."

As though she knew exactly what he needed, Sam continued to whisper as he began moving, sliding inside of her, pulling back. Slowly. Ever so slowly. He didn't try to increase the pace for fear he'd go off like a rocket.

But then their bodies became one. They were moving together, his mouth finding hers. The kiss scorched him, a conflagration that disintegrated any and all thought.

"Harder, Eli. Yes," Sam moaned. "Just. Like. That."

Sam's words were punctuated by his thrusts, which had increased in tempo to the point he couldn't slow down. He didn't want to slow down. She felt so good. Soft, warm ... Sam.

"Baby," he groaned. "Sam... God, I'm not going to last. Oh, Sam." Her internal muscles squeezed him and Elijah saw stars. He began thrusting his hips harder, faster, his mouth crushing to hers, one hand in her hair as he held her.

"Eli!" Sam moaned his name, and Elijah swallowed her cry, driving into her over and over, their bodies slick with perspiration.

They broke the kiss, the need for air forcing them apart, and when their eyes met again, brown locked to green, Elijah knew this was it for him. He'd purposely kept himself locked away, his heart secured in a tiny black box that would allow no one else to penetrate it.

But right here, tonight ... this woman... She effectively shattered that box, his heart swelling, emotion nearly consuming him.

Reaching between them, Elijah pressed his thumb against her clit, gently massaging in circles until Sam was crying out, begging for him to never stop.

"Eli! I'm coming!"

"Sam. Oh, God, Sam." And with that, Elijah followed her over, his release detonating.

And what do you know ... that was the night he learned that his heart was big enough to love both Beth and Sam.

# CHAPTER SEVENTEEN

THE FIRST GOLDEN RAYS OF THE SUN were creeping through the blinds as Sam lay against Elijah, her hand circling over the light dusting of dark hair over his chest.

After they'd made love, they had spent a couple of hours talking, holding on to one another as though this were both their first and their last night together. And now, as dawn broke, they'd been asleep for hours, but Sam had awoken to find Elijah gone. At first, she'd been worried, but he had returned moments later with a sheepish grin.

"Nature called."

Sam had laughed, and when he'd crawled back in bed, she'd curled up against him once again. Which was where she was now. The heat of his body pressed up against her, his even breaths grazing her hair. For the better part of the last few minutes, Sam had been thinking about Logan. And Elijah. Both of them together.

And how much she missed Logan. She didn't like when he went off on his business trips, but luckily, they were few and far between. She was hoping he would call to let her know he was on his way soon.

"Are you all right?" Elijah asked, his fingers gliding along her upper arm.

"Yeah. You?"

"Never better."

Sam pushed up onto her elbow and turned to look at Elijah, wanting to see his face when he made an admission such as that one.

"At least not in a very long time," he added, his eyes hooded.

"Are you thinking about Beth?" she asked.

"I'm always thinking about her," he said sadly.

"I can't begin to imagine how you feel, but I'm glad that you can hang on to the memories. I think she would like knowing that you think about her."

"I talk to her sometimes."

Sam smiled. "I bet she really likes that." The sadness she saw in his eyes tore at her heart.

"On our tenth wedding anniversary, I stayed home," he began, his voice soft. "It was me and a bottle of Jack Daniels. We hung out all night. I went through our wedding album and every picture ever taken of her or both of us. I talked to her that night more than I ever have."

Sam's heart constricted. She could picture this strong, confident, handsome man sitting in a dark, empty house on what would've been his tenth anniversary with the woman he loved. God, it must've been terrible.

"Do you go visit her grave?" Sam asked, keeping her voice as quiet as his had been.

"Not as much as I should. I try to take flowers every few months."

Sam continued to watch him for a moment. When he finally met her gaze, she said, "The next time you go, I'd like to go with you. If you don't mind."

Sam could've sworn she saw tears form in his golden eyes, but they were quickly gone as he pulled her closer, forcing her on top of him. Rather than answer her, he kissed her. It was sweet and hot and … she was panting before they came up for air.

She pushed up so that she could reach over to the night table, where another condom was sitting. She reached for it, but she didn't move to put it on him. Yet. The entire time, Elijah watched her, his face a mix of emotions. So many, Sam had no clue what he was thinking or feeling.

"Logan told me he wanted to watch us like this," she whispered, feeling a little daring now that she was straddling him.

"Did he?" Elijah asked, a small smile lighting up his face.

"Yes," she answered. "He said he wanted to watch while I rode you."

"Do you wish he was here, Sam?" Elijah asked, somewhat seriously.

"Yes," she admitted openly. "I do. Last night was incredible. Don't get me wrong. But I would love for Logan to be here. He completes me. The same way Beth completes you."

A noise near the door caught Sam's attention, and she turned to see Logan standing there. He had on a black polo and faded jeans, and holy shit, he looked so good.

"Logan," Sam whispered, unable to hide her excitement.

"I still want to watch, but right now, I'd prefer to join in," Logan said, his voice gruff, his eyes sparkling.

He'd heard everything she'd said.

Sam glanced back at Elijah, and she realized he'd asked that question on purpose. He'd known that Logan was standing there. And he had known without asking what her answer was.

With that single question, he had made everything right.

Smiling down at Elijah, Sam decided it was time to thank him.

LOGAN HAD BEEN STANDING IN THE DOORWAY for less than a minute. He'd come into the house and gone straight to his bedroom. And when he'd gotten to the door, he'd come to a complete stop. His bed was made; there weren't any clothes on the floor, which meant one of two things. Either Sam had gone back to Elijah's after all, or they'd ... they were in the guest bedroom.

His heart felt lighter knowing that Sam and Elijah hadn't been in their bed.

When he had been able to convince his feet to move, Logan had gone toward the guest bedroom, and sure enough, the moment he'd laid eyes on Samantha straddling Elijah's narrow hips, his blood pressure had ratcheted up a few notches.

But that wasn't what had nearly done him in. It was Samantha's admission that had his heart pounding.

Blinking several times to clear his eyes because, hell no, he would not fucking cry, Logan focused on the couple across the room.

"Give me a minute," he told them and made a hasty retreat to his bedroom to grab the bottle of lube that they would certainly need in a few minutes.

Once he returned, after taking several steps into the room, Logan didn't try to be quiet. He was here to participate. He'd been hard as steel ever since he'd received that phone call from Elijah the night before. Just imagining what the two of them had been doing had made him crazy with lust. Sure, there'd been a few other emotions mixed in there, too, but after hearing Sam's truthful admission, his fear had disappeared.

Only a tremendous amount of love for this woman.

That's all that was left.

Oh, and lust.

Definitely lust.

Kicking off his shoes, Logan reached behind his head and yanked his shirt off in one easy move. He then went to work on his jeans.

Once he was as naked as they were, Logan stood at the side of the bed, stroking his cock while he watched them. Sam was watching him, a wide smile on her face, her eyes glistening a little, too.

"My turn," Logan said, his eyes darting down to Elijah, who hadn't moved yet.

Elijah must've known what Logan wanted because he held out his hand for the lube at the same time he snatched the condom from Sam's hands, making her laugh.

"In a hurry?"

"Have you seen what you look like?" Logan asked. "It's fucking hot to watch you straddle him like that. I missed out on the action last night, so yeah, I'm in a bit of a hurry."

Sam laughed again, this time making Elijah, who'd been suiting and slicking up, laugh also. And when Elijah pulled Sam, somehow managing to flip her over so that she was on her back on top of him, Logan stopped breathing.

With her legs spread wide for him, Elijah's thick cock rigid and heavy right there between her thighs, Logan had to fight to maintain control.

"Ride me, Sam," Elijah told her, and that's when Sam realized just what he was talking about. Her eyes widened as she looked up at Logan.

Logan kneeled on the bed and reached for her, taking her hands as she sat up on her knees facing him. Elijah was still prone on the bed, Sam kneeling above him but facing the opposite direction, giving Elijah the perfect opportunity to...

Logan crushed his mouth to Sam's as Elijah began guiding his lubed cock into her ass. Logan wasn't gentle as he fondled her nipples, sucking on her tongue, nipping her bottom lip, all while she moaned from the mix of pleasure and pain.

"Fuck!" Elijah growled, his voice strained.

Logan knew just what he was feeling.

"So tight."

"Logan," Sam pleaded, and he realized he'd pulled back to get a better view.

"That's it, baby. Eli's going to fuck your ass while I drive deep into your pussy. You want that? Me fucking you hard and fast while Elijah's buried inside you?"

"Yes," she moaned.

"Come here, Sam," Elijah said through gritted teeth.

Logan helped Elijah pull her down so that she was lying flush against him, her back to his chest.

"That's fucking hot, baby," Logan told her as he shifted so that he could position himself between their spread legs.

The bed was king-sized, but it wasn't all that easy for the three of them, especially Logan, whose height hindered his ability to get comfortable. Realizing he was going to have to get off the bed to make it work, Logan did just that.

He came around to the end of the bed, but rather than climb back on, he leaned forward, spreading Sam's pussy lips and sliding his tongue through her slick folds. He concentrated on her clit while Elijah began pumping his hips, driving himself into her but unable to retreat much due to the fact Sam was lying on top of him.

Sam cried out, her hand yanking on his hair as she tried to pull him up her body. Logan looked up at her and smiled. "In a hurry?" He returned her words to her and she laughed.

"Yes. God, yes."

Yeah, he was, too.

Elijah groaned. "Don't make her laugh," he bit out through clenched teeth. "She'll make me come."

Logan laughed again, unable to help himself.

Crawling onto the bed, Logan knelt between their legs, using his knees to push Elijah's open a little wider to give him more room. Once he was situated, he stroked his cock, lining it up with the entrance to Sam's warm, wet heat.

Fuck.

He slid in slowly. Or at least as slow as he could manage because, yes, she was fucking hot. And tight. The fact that Elijah was lodged in her ass only added to the sensation, the heavy ridge of his erection sliding alongside Logan's.

"Fuck," Elijah growled, his hands wrapping around Sam, holding her tight. "Fuck her, Logan."

He didn't need to be told twice.

Meeting Sam's gaze, Logan said, "I'm going to fuck you, baby. Hard and fast. Understand?"

"Yes, please. Quit talking," she said with a strangled laugh, eliciting another tortured groan from Elijah.

Logan drove into her all the way, bottoming out and catching his breath before retreating. He leaned over Sam and Elijah, doing his best not to crush her between them as he began pounding into her, rocking her body so that she was impaled on Elijah's cock buried deep in her ass.

"Does it feel good?" he asked, breathless.

"Yes. Fuck me, Logan. Fuck me harder!"

Logan didn't hesitate, his hands fisting the blankets beneath them as he began slamming into her, over and over, faster, harder, deeper. Fucking hell.

Sam cried out, her pussy milking him, nearly pulling his own orgasm from him. Somehow he managed to refrain, not wanting to come yet. Not until Elijah was there, until all three of them could go together.

Rising back to his knees, Logan grabbed Sam's ankles. "Pull your knees against your chest," he told her.

She managed to pull her knees in closer, which allowed Elijah the ability to thrust his hips, shallowly driving into her. Logan assisted by slamming into her. He released one of her ankles so he could play with her clit, strumming it with his thumb while she moaned and writhed, attempting to help them along.

"Close," Elijah said, his voice muffled. "So fucking close. Damn, baby. Sam... Oh, fuck."

Elijah's hips stilled, his dick pulsing, and Logan upped the tempo, slamming into her again and again, driving himself as deep as he could. He met Sam's hooded eyes.

"Logan! Oh, God, Logan. I'm..."

Yeah, he was, too.

# CHAPTER EIGHTEEN

*Two weeks later...*

FOR THE PAST TWO WEEKS, SAM HAD spent a lot of time with both Logan and Elijah. Together. Separate. But no matter what, she'd had at least one of them with her. Well, except for the night she'd gone out with the girls, but even then, she'd talked about them so much it'd felt as though they'd been right there with her.

To put it mildly, the last few weeks had been the most amazing weeks of her life. The three of them were getting close. Closer than she'd thought they would. Elijah and Logan spent time together, as well, much of the time right there at the house just talking. They had a lot in common and not just work.

Sam didn't think it could get better than it was.

But that thought was the very reason she was sitting on the sofa, her phone in her hand while Logan was in their master bathroom showering. She needed to call Elijah because there was something on her mind that she couldn't seem to shake.

Before she could muster the courage to dial, her phone startled her when it started ringing in her hand. She glanced down at the screen to see Elijah's name come up. Taking a deep breath, she hit the talk button.

"Did you know I was thinking about you?" she asked as a greeting.

"No," Elijah said and she noticed a sadness in his tone. "But it makes me feel good to know that."

"What's wrong?" she asked, all teasing aside.

"I just needed to hear your voice this morning," he said, and Sam's heart did a somersault in her chest.

They were both quiet for a moment, and finally Sam decided to spill it. "What are you doing today?"

"Nothing that I know of," he told her.

"I was wondering if..." Sam choked on the words.

"What is it, Sam? Is everything okay?"

"Everything's fine. Mostly. God, this is going to sound really stupid, but I wanted to see if we could go visit Beth today."

Elijah didn't say anything, which made Sam panic. "If you don't want to, I completely understand. It's just that I wanted to, you know, go talk to her. I thought..."

"I'd love that," Elijah finally said, his voice much softer than before.

"How about we come to you. Logan and I will meet you at your house. Then we'll go over there together. Will that work?"

"Yes. That works."

"We'll be there in half an hour. Or do you need more time?"

"I'll be ready. Oh, and ... thank you, Sam."

Sam didn't know what he was thanking her for, but the phone disconnected, and she was left sitting there alone. When she looked up, she saw Logan watching her. That's when she realized she was crying.

"Does he want to go?" Logan asked.

"Yes," she answered. "I told him we'd be there in half an hour."

Logan nodded and returned to the bedroom, probably to get his shoes.

It had been Logan's suggestion to go to the gravesite. They'd been talking, just the two of them, the night before, and she had mentioned how she wished she could've met Beth. It was a strange emotion for her, she knew, but she felt a connection to the woman. Obviously through Elijah. And for some reason, she wanted a chance to let Beth know that she was there. To let the woman who would forever hold Elijah's heart know that she wanted to be the person who would take care of Elijah for her.

Because, yes, that's what Sam wanted.

Because, yes, she had fallen in love with the man.

And in turn, her love for Logan had only intensified. She needed him more than ever, and he seemed to know that. Then again, he seemed to know that Elijah needed him, too. They'd become friends in the past few weeks. Sam knew they talked, knew that Logan always offered to be an ear for Elijah should he need it. And, possibly because of Logan, Elijah had been opening up more.

He spent more time out of his house, hanging with them or with an entire group. They'd gone to dinner several times, once with Ashleigh and Alex, once with Luke, Sierra, and Cole. They'd also gone to the club, spent some time talking to Xander and Mercedes. All of them.

And as the days passed, people seemed to be seeing them as three, not just two plus one. And that made Sam's heart happy.

So now she felt that there was one thing left to do. Because Elijah had sought Logan's approval, Sam wanted to show Elijah that she understood what that meant.

Now it was her turn.

---

THE SUN WAS SHINING.

A gentle breeze was blowing.

But other than that, time seemed to stand still as Elijah stood in front of Beth's headstone, two dozen white roses — her favorite — now resting next to the inscription.

Upon their arrival a short while ago, the three of them had emerged from the car, but as soon as they'd stepped outside, Sam and Logan had stayed back, offering him a few minutes alone with Beth.

How they had known that he needed that, he wasn't sure. But he appreciated it nonetheless.

"God, baby," he whispered to Beth now, tears forming in his eyes. "I miss you so much." Elijah paused as a strong breeze pushed against him.

Sometimes he felt as though that was Beth's way of responding to him, letting him know she was there. It only happened when he was out here with her, though.

"I brought someone here to meet you. Two someones, actually. Logan and Samantha. This was their idea. For them to come here. Sam really wants to meet you." Elijah was crying, tears streaming down his face, and he couldn't stop them.

He'd been totally overcome with emotion since Sam had asked him if the three of them could come to visit Beth. At first he'd been shocked by the invitation but only because he had called her, simply to hear her voice. For the last two days, he had been out of town, and with as much time as the three of them had been spending together, he'd found that he'd missed her. Enough to call her just to hear her voice.

Another breeze brushed against him, stronger this time. Elijah looked up, expecting to see clouds, maybe a thunderhead moving toward them. Nothing. Not a single cloud in the brilliant blue sky that went on for miles.

He turned his attention back to Beth.

"Sam's the best thing that's happened to me since you died," he told Beth now.

A strong hand landed on Elijah's left shoulder, and he felt Logan's presence. On his other side, Sam moved up next to him, but she didn't touch him. He figured she was giving him space, but he didn't want space. Not from her. He reached out and took her hand, linking their fingers as he continued to stare at his wife's headstone.

Elizabeth Michelle Penn
June 2, 1973 - January 17, 2010

*You will forever be in my heart,*
*Your love always my guide,*
*And though I cannot touch your hand,*
*I know you are by my side*

"THAT'S A LOVELY INSCRIPTION," SAM WHISPERED, HER fingers tightening around his.

"It's true," he told her now. "She's here with me. She'll always be here with me."

"We're glad you are here with him, Beth. He needs you... And we need him."

Elijah closed his eyes, trying to stop the tears, but he couldn't seem to shut off the waterworks. He couldn't look at Sam or Logan, his watery gaze focused on the headstone. Sam's words echoed in his head, *and we need him*. He needed them, too, but he was too scared to tell them. Especially here.

An even stronger breeze cut through them, and Elijah tightened his grip on Sam's fingers.

If that wasn't Beth, it was certainly an eerie coincidence. And if it was, Elijah only prayed that was her blessing because ... he was pretty sure he was not going to be able to let Sam go. Not today. Not ever.

LOGAN REMAINED QUIET, ALTHOUGH HE KEPT HIS hand on Elijah's shoulder, letting him know that he was there.

He had known that this was going to be an emotional reunion, and it was. Especially now that Sam was talking to Beth. He would've thought it strange that the two of them were talking to a dead woman, but Logan had done the same. Many times.

He'd spent years talking to his parents after they'd died. And when his grandfather had passed away, he'd done the same with him. It wasn't until Sam had come along and mended his heart with her love that he had stopped.

He doubted Elijah would ever stop. And he understood that, too. That connection, once established, would not be severed. Didn't matter if it were distance or death, the heart would never let go. For those who were blessed to know or to have known the type of love that Elijah and Beth shared, the same type of love that Logan and Sam shared, they knew it was forever.

Regardless of circumstance.

Logan's attention was diverted when Sam moved. She walked behind Elijah and then inserted herself between them, her arms around them both. Logan dropped his hand from Elijah's shoulder and held Sam.

The three of them stood in silence for a few minutes, and then Elijah turned to them, a gentle smile on his face.

"What do you say we get out of here?"

Logan nodded, releasing Sam as she turned toward the car.

"Can we go to dinner?" she asked, looking between the two of them.

"I'd like that," Elijah said, his eyes meeting Logan's.

If he wasn't mistaken, there was a measure of peace in Elijah's eyes. And despite the tears that he'd silently shed, Logan got the impression that Elijah was breathing a little easier.

# CHAPTER NINETEEN

*One week later...*

SAM WAS SITTING ON A LOUNGE CHAIR by the pool. The temperature hovered in the upper eighties, but the gentle breeze made it bearable. She'd opened one of the umbrellas to shield herself from the brutal rays of the sun as she sat quietly. Reflecting.

That's what she'd been doing since the moment Elijah had left that morning.

He had, for the first time since they'd visited Beth's grave, spent the night with them. They had ended up falling asleep in the guest room, Logan on one side, Elijah on the other, while she'd slept in between them.

Last night had been... God, she didn't know what it had been, but she almost felt as though Elijah was trying to pull away when, for the last few weeks, they'd all been growing closer. Yet last night had been emotional. Yes, that was the word.

She hadn't wanted him to go, but she had known at the time that he needed some space. So, she'd let him walk away. And after he'd left, Logan had pulled her into his arms and held her. It'd taken her a good half hour to find the strength to pull away from her husband, but she'd finally managed.

At that point, Logan had gone about his day, a lazy Sunday like most Sundays, and Sam had gone to do her thing. There was no lingering tension, nothing that should've drawn attention to last night being any different from any other night they'd spent together.

But her thoughts drifted to Elijah. She wished he were there. She wanted him there. Even if he were just sitting in the house, reading or watching television, whatever he did on a Sunday afternoon when there was nothing on the calendar. That's the only thing that seemed to be missing. At least for her.

"Hey." Logan's voice broke through her thoughts, and Sam shielded her eyes as she glanced up at him. He was holding a glass of iced tea, which she took from his hand.

"Thank you."

"What's on your mind, baby?" he asked as he squatted down beside her, his hand settling warmly on hers.

"Elijah," she admitted.

Logan didn't say anything and Sam didn't know what to say. They stared back at one another as though they were both trying to figure out what the next steps were but wanting the other one to make the decision.

Finally, Sam said, "Where do we go from here?"

Logan shifted, sitting on the edge of her lounge chair. He took the glass of tea from her hands and set it on the table beside the chair. "That depends. We need to talk to Elijah."

"This is moving so quickly," she told him. "It's only been like, what, a month? But I..." Sam clamped her mouth shut, tears suddenly springing to her eyes as she realized what she was about to say.

"You love him," Logan said. It wasn't phrased as a question, because her husband knew. He knew just how much she had come to care about Elijah.

"Yeah," she whispered, a sob breaking free. "Does that make me a bad person?"

Logan reached for her, wrapping his big arms around her, holding her against him, and Sam went freely. She grabbed on to him, holding tightly.

"I love you, Logan. I love you more than anything in the world. My life would never be complete without you."

She was rambling, her tears wetting his T-shirt, but he didn't pull away from her.

"I know that, baby. I've never doubted your love for me."

Sam released him, pushing away so she could look at him. "Doesn't that bother you? That I said I love another man?"

Logan's eyes softened. "I heard what you told Elijah, Sam. Remember when you told him that I complete you the way Beth completes him? Well, the same for me. You complete me. And God, that sounds so cliché, but it's true. I also know how much you love me. You don't even have to say it for me to feel it. I feel it," he said, two long fingers thumping the area over his heart, "right here."

"It just…" Sam looked away. "It's all happened so fast. We just met him a month ago, and suddenly I love him?"

"There's no time table, Sam. You can't fit love into a schedule, remember? You've got to let that go. Think of it this way… Maybe it's been a long time. We've been waiting for Elijah. And now he's here and we can move forward."

"How do we move forward?"

"You need to tell him how you feel," Logan answered. "Then we need to decide what we want to do from here. Do we make this more … permanent?"

"Like him moving in with us?" Sam asked because, yes, she'd been thinking about that when Logan had come outside. She wanted Elijah there with them. She wanted him close so she could take care of him. She hated to think about him sitting at home alone with his thoughts. She wanted to be able to talk to him.

"Yes. I think that's the next step. Maybe not today or tomorrow, but I think it's something we need to discuss with him."

"Do you think he'll want that?"

"That's not a question I can answer. And you'll never know until you ask him, Sam."

Sitting up straight, Sam allowed Logan to see everything she was feeling. Yes, she was confused, but more than that, she was happy.

"Will you take me to see him?"

"Whenever you're ready."

Sam didn't even need to say anything more before Logan chuckled. "Have I told you how hot you are when you're in a hurry?"

Getting to her feet, Sam grabbed the glass of iced tea from the table and faced off with Logan again. "Yes, but feel free to tell me again."

---

SUNDAY AFTERNOON WASN'T QUITE AS EVENTFUL AS Sunday morning had been. At least not for Elijah.

After Sam had woken him with her wicked mouth and after she'd done the same to Logan, the three of them had opted for a shower. Elijah would admit he was rather impressed with Logan and Sam's shower. It was big enough for an orgy. And since there were only three of them, it had left a significant amount of room for them to enjoy themselves. Namely, Elijah and Logan, who'd both had the pleasure of thoroughly washing Sam until she was coming again. Twice.

The woman was so damned responsive, and if he weren't mistaken, she wanted sex as much as they did. Maybe more. And no, Elijah wasn't complaining.

Not even a little.

However, after their shower, Elijah had informed them he needed to go home. It had been a lie, but neither of them had pushed him, so he'd called a cab.

But now that he was home, he wished he were back at Sam's. Elijah hadn't been a big fan of his lonely house before Sam had brought the sunshine back into his life, but now he found that he dreaded being there.

He just wasn't sure what he was supposed to do about that.

After rummaging through the refrigerator to find there wasn't a damn thing in the house to make for dinner, Elijah settled on a glass of his favorite scotch. Glass in hand, he returned to the living room and went to stand in front of the fireplace.

He rested his hand on the mantel, his fingers touching the edge of one of the shiny frames that held his most precious possessions. Sipping his drink, he just stared back at the image in front of him.

"Beth." He whispered his wife's name as he stared back at the picture of her bright, smiling face.

He missed her. He hadn't talked to her since they'd gone to her grave. He'd been scared to. Scared to reveal what he knew to be true.

*"Do you wish he was here, Sam?" Elijah asked Sam.*

*"Yes, I do. Last night was incredible, don't get me wrong. But I would love for Logan to be here. He completes me. The same way Beth completes you."*

That conversation he'd had with Sam always ran through his head. He was pretty sure it had been then that he'd fallen head-over-heels in love with the woman. The easy way she had admitted to needing Logan had settled something inside of Elijah. She understood him better than he even understood himself. She didn't seem to mind that she would forever share him with Beth. And as soon as the words had left her mouth, he'd had to swallow past the lump of emotion that had knotted in his throat.

He loved her. Sam. He loved her, too.

Yes, he would admit, he'd fallen for Sam. He hadn't expected it; hell, he hadn't actually thought it possible, but here he was, in love with a woman who was not his wife.

Did that mean he loved Beth any less? No, it didn't. And that felt good. Incredibly good.

"I love you, Beth. You know that, right?" he spoke to the picture of her from their wedding day. It was one of those candid shots that had frozen a moment in time when Beth had been smiling, her eyes lit up. She was the only one in the picture, but Elijah remembered that moment. She'd been talking to him, smiling at him. Loving him.

"I'll never stop, Beth. I swear to you. I will never stop loving you. But I... God, Beth, I... I've fallen in love with her, and I don't know what the hell I'm supposed to do about that."

"Tell her."

Elijah nearly dropped his now empty glass as he turned to see Samantha standing in his living room. Behind her was Logan, both of them staring back at him.

"How'd..." That wasn't really important.

"Your front door was unlocked. We knocked, but..." Sam let her explanation drift off, as she, too, must've realized that it wasn't important how she had gotten in there.

Just the fact that she was there was all that mattered.

Turning back to look at Beth's picture, Elijah placed his glass on the mantel as he took a deep breath. When he turned back, Sam was closer. Just a foot away from him.

"I didn't expect this," he said by way of excuse, talking fast. "I just didn't. When I met Logan at X-hale—"

"Tell me," Sam said firmly, her hand settling on his arm as she took another step closer. "I don't need reasons, Eli. Just tell me."

Elijah could see tears in her eyes, and the thought of her crying broke his heart. He looked back at Logan over Sam's head, and the man nodded.

"I love you, Sam. I don't know how that happened, and I—"

"I love you, too," Sam whispered. "As I was subtly reminded a short while ago, love doesn't pay attention to time. It can happen suddenly." Sam glanced past Elijah to the picture on the mantle. "And it can last for eternity."

Elijah reached for her, unable to stop himself. When she walked into his arms, he wrapped himself around her, holding her tight. He stared back at Logan.

"It's true," Logan confirmed. "We can't predict how things will happen. And no amount of excuses or reasons will change it. So from this moment forward, we just need to accept this for what it is. Everyone else be damned. This is what we want."

*We.*

Elijah liked the sound of that. He couldn't find the words to say, so he nodded, fully understanding.

As much as he loved Sam, as grateful as he was to have her in his life, Elijah had also developed a bond with Logan. They were friends. They loved the same woman. And they entrusted one another with her. There would never be a single moment when Sam didn't know just how much she was wanted. They would both make sure of that.

"So where do we go from here?" Elijah asked, letting up on the stranglehold he had on Sam. She didn't move away, just looked up at him.

"That's what we're here to ask you," Sam answered, her face radiant, her smile brilliant.

She warmed him completely. His heart. His body. His soul.

"Well, since we've gone at warp speed thus far, I really don't see the need to slow down. Do you?" Elijah asked.

Sam shook her head.

"Full speed ahead it is then," Elijah said, pulling Sam close as he kissed her.

And a second later, Logan joined them.

# CHAPTER TWENTY

*The next day...*

To say she was nervous would be a huge understatement.

To say she was excited would be one, as well.

Sam didn't quite know what to feel, but watching Elijah and Logan talking quietly was making her body tremble, and she wasn't sure if that was a good thing or a bad thing.

At first, she had attempted to distract herself by watching the room where Xander and Mercedes were. As she'd watched, Xander had strapped her to a St. Andrew's cross, and for a fraction of a second, she had envisioned herself in that woman's place.

The fantasy had festered only briefly before she'd turned her attention to Logan and Elijah, who appeared to be deep in conversation. She had no idea what they were talking about, but she hoped it was about her.

Now, as she tried to focus on Xander once again, she found her attention span was equivalent to that of a gnat. She was tired of watching others. She wanted to participate.

Not that she wanted to be on full display in one of the glass rooms as Mercedes now was. No, she much preferred the private room that Elijah had alluded to a few minutes ago. They had been talking to Sierra and Cole shortly after they'd arrived, but then her two men had led her away, and she had believed they were ready to go to that private room, but apparently, a detour had been necessary.

Which left her standing there, watching the scene before her while she waited for Logan and Elijah to figure it out. Whatever *it* was.

Her skin felt too tight, her body too hot. Excitement fizzed in her veins, and she was anxious to see what they had in store for her.

Just when she thought she was going to lose her mind, a solid body pressed up against her and a familiar scent assaulted her.

Logan.

God, he smelled good.

His hands came to rest on her hips as he leaned down, his mouth close to her ear.

"Are you ready?" he asked.

Sam didn't need to ask him to clarify. She knew he was referring to their conversation from late last night. The three of them had been lying in bed — in the guest room they'd reserved for their threesome time — discussing the whole BDSM experimentation. More accurately, Elijah and Logan had been going on and on about the swing. Apparently, they both wanted one for the house.

And since they didn't have one yet, Elijah was quite anxious to try it out. She assumed that's what they would be doing.

"Yes," she confirmed, not moving from her spot.

"Good. Elijah's got a private room upstairs. It's ready and waiting for us."

Relief flooded her.

She was always wary of Logan's desire to use one of the glass rooms. It wasn't that she was opposed to an audience, but she much preferred at least a little privacy. Especially since she was already nervous about what the two of them were going to do to her.

"Elijah will be here in a minute. He's going to take you upstairs." Logan pressed his lips to her ear. "I'm going to watch, just like I said I wanted to. I want to see you strapped to that swing while Elijah drives his cock deep into your pussy."

A full-body shudder assaulted her.

Watching. Her husband would be watching her with Elijah.

Not that he hadn't plenty of times in recent weeks, but generally, he joined right in, using the excuse that he just couldn't stay away from her.

The idea made her pussy throb.

She didn't ask him to continue because she was too anxious to get on with it. Logan planted a quick kiss on her neck before he backed away, leaving her standing there, watching Xander do wicked things to Mercedes.

Another warm body pressed up against her, and this time she knew it wasn't Logan. Her husband's body was familiar; this one was very familiar, too.

"Come with me, baby," Elijah whispered against her ear, his accent and his deep voice causing goose bumps to rise on her skin.

Elijah took her hand in his, leading her to the stairs that would take them to one of the more private rooms on the second floor. She didn't hesitate, even though she did glance around, trying to spot Logan. She didn't find him, but she knew he was there, watching her.

Elijah stopped in front of a closed door, turning to face her. He startled her when he pulled her into him, crushing his mouth to hers. God, the man could kiss. Like a dream.

"What was that for?" she asked in breathless anticipation when he pulled back.

"Mmm, just wanted to taste you."

Sam knew they'd caught the attention of a few of the members. She could feel their eyes on them.

"And I wanted everyone to know you were here with me, too," Elijah whispered against her mouth.

Sam smiled. She couldn't help herself.

"But now, I want you all to myself." Taking her hand, he opened the door with his free hand and pulled her inside abruptly, making her laugh at his excitement.

Yep, there it was.

That swing.

It didn't look quite as intimidating as it had the last time she'd seen it.

"I remember the last time you were here," Elijah told her. "I think you were made to fit in that damn thing. So fucking hot, Sam."

Another shiver of anticipation raced through her. Yeah, she had been excited about this ever since Elijah and Logan had given her a graphic depiction of the scene from their point of view.

"Turn around," Elijah told her, his tone commanding.

Hmm, she liked that.

Turning away from him, Sam waited with bated breath for him to move along. They'd been teasing her relentlessly since they'd arrived, and now that they were there, in the room, she was quickly running out of patience.

Oh, who was she kidding? She didn't have any patience to begin with.

Sam felt the gentle touch of Elijah's hands as he pushed her hair over her shoulder. The zipper on her dress being lowered was the only sound aside from her rapid breathing.

"Did I mention I like this dress?"

"You did," she answered. "More than once."

"Well, I'm telling you again. I like this dress. I happen to like it when it is on you, but I like it even more when it is on the floor at your feet."

This particular dress was strapless, so she didn't have to move for him to get the fabric to slide down her body. Unlike last time she'd encountered this swing, Sam did have on her panties and bra.

And to her delight, Elijah took his time removing those, his hands fondling her as he went along.

"Good thing Logan gave me a brief rundown on how this thing works," Elijah said as he reached around her, squeezing her now naked breasts.

"I assume you're referring to the swing?" she asked teasingly.

He pinched her nipples simultaneously, making her shriek. The pain-filled pleasure was erotic as hell.

"Yes, wildcat, that's what I'm referring to."

*Wildcat?* She kinda liked that.

Elijah put his hands on her hips, guiding her toward the swing and then turning her so that she faced him.

Apparently Logan had been thorough in his instruction, because a few minutes later, Sam was strapped firmly in the swing while Elijah took a step back, apparently admiring his handiwork.

She only hoped he admired faster because she was ready.

More than ready.

---

YEAH, ELIJAH WOULD HAVE TO AGREE WITH Logan. This swing was a must-have. He had no idea where the hell they'd put it, but he wasn't opposed to finding a place. As far as he was concerned, right in the middle of the kitchen would work just fine.

Especially if he could come home from work to find Sam strapped in and ready.

Fuck.

He was watching her now, well aware of the impatience brimming inside of her. She was hot and bothered, but then again, they'd been purposely working to arouse her for the better part of the evening.

It had been her idea to come to the club, after all, so it was only fair. At least in his opinion. She'd made the suggestion after their stimulating discussion about this very swing that morning. Who were they to refuse her?

Moving forward, Elijah used the tips of his fingers to brush over her engorged clit, sliding down through the moisture that coated her pretty pussy. She was definitely ready.

"I like you restrained like that," he told her honestly. "I think we should try this more often."

"The swing?" she asked, her words clipped from her excitement.

"A bed works fine, too. I just like you laid out for me."

Sam closed her eyes, her head falling back when he drove two fingers into her. "Eli..."

"Yes, baby?"

"Make me come..." Sam breathed in deep. "Please."

"With my fingers?"

"I really don't care... Oh, God!"

Elijah used his other hand to tease her clit while he slowly fucked her with two fingers.

"Or with my mouth?" he asked as he lowered himself to his knees between her thighs. Logan had been right; the swing was just the right height so that he could easily eat her pussy while he was kneeling.

"Eli!" Sam groaned long and deep when he used his fingers to separate her folds, delicately tracing her puffy pink lips. He leaned forward and circled her clit with his tongue over and over until she was repeating his name in a rush.

He'd restrained her arms, unlike the last time when he'd watched Logan fuck her in this swing. And that meant she couldn't reach for him and she couldn't rock the swing to get what she wanted, leaving him in complete control.

He took full advantage of the control.

Feasting on her pussy, Elijah didn't even hear the door open, but he felt Logan as he moved inside. The man wasn't in a hurry, and he didn't make his way over to them right away.

"Logan!" Sam cried out. "I need to come!"

"Is he tormenting you, baby?"

"Yes... Oh, God, yes. Don't stop, Eli. Please don't stop!"

Elijah had no intention of stopping. He loved eating her pussy, driving his tongue inside, alternating with his fingers. She loved it, too; he had no doubt about that.

Logan moved into his line of sight, up toward Sam's head. "I'm going to lower this a little," Logan said. Elijah wasn't sure whom he was talking to, nor did he care.

Elijah watched them as he fucked Sam with his fingers while he teased her clit with his tongue. Logan had lowered her head a little. He had pulled his cock out, stroking it slowly as he stood beside her head.

"I thought you were just going to watch," Sam teased, breathlessly.

"Yeah, well, you should never believe me when I say that. Suck me, Sam. I want to watch my dick fuck your pretty mouth."

Sam turned to face Logan. His cock disappeared inside of Sam's hungry mouth a moment later as her pussy clamped down on Elijah's fingers. She loved this. She loved being the focus of two men.

Elijah loved it, too.

"Suck me deeper, baby," Logan encouraged. "I want you to come, but only when you make me come. Understand? That's it. Fuck, that feels good."

Logan was fondling his balls with one hand while Sam was taking his dick deep in her mouth. Since she was unable to use her hands, Logan could control the depth and speed. Elijah finger fucked her in perfect rhythm to Logan's cock tunneling in and out of her mouth.

"Oh, fuck, baby," Logan groaned, his hand tightening on her hair. "Just like that. Fuck yeah. I'm gonna come in your mouth. Are you ready?"

Logan glanced over at Elijah for the first time, a wordless signal, and Elijah sucked her clit into his mouth, as he thrust his fingers in deep, pulled them out, back in deeper. This time he didn't pull out; instead he twisted, applying pressure right ... there.

Sam screamed, the sound muffled by Logan's cock buried in her mouth. Her pussy clamped on to his fingers, her clit pulsing against his lips as her body shuddered.

"Fuck yes," Logan groaned, his hips stilling, his attention once again on Sam's face as he came in her mouth.

---

LOGAN'S COCK WAS SPENT, BUT HE KNEW Sam was nowhere near close to being done. Nor was Elijah.

Tucking his cock into his pants but not bothering to zip up, he adjusted the nylon straps so that Sam's head was raised somewhat. Elijah was already on his feet, stroking his cock as he reached for a condom.

Logan looked at Sam. She looked back at him.

"Eli," Sam said. "I... I want to feel you."

"I'm hurrying, baby," he responded, clearly misunderstanding the meaning of Sam's statement.

"No. I mean, I want to feel you. Just you. Nothing between us."

Elijah's eyebrows rose as he looked back at Sam. His usually bright brown eyes darkened. He definitely understood what she meant that time.

"We're safe," Sam told him. "I'm on birth control and we've all been tested. We want this, Eli."

Logan was trying to make sense of Sam's words, trying to understand why she was seemingly trying to talk him into this.

Elijah looked back at Logan. "Not since Beth have I not used a condom. I..."

"We want this," Logan assured him, suddenly realizing. Elijah hadn't had sex without a condom with anyone other than his wife. And that made this a big deal for him.

Elijah stroked himself vigorously as he moved back to Sam. He looked on the verge of losing it, but then, without preamble, Elijah slid home.

"Fuck," Elijah growled. "God, it feels too good." Elijah didn't move for the longest time.

Logan took a step back, not wanting to get in their way, when Elijah began to pump his hips. He thought back to the first night Elijah had joined them in this very room. Logan had been where Elijah was now. And yes, he could see just how fucking hot it was to watch Sam being fucked. Hard.

And that's what Elijah was doing. He was pounding into Sam, her moans filling the room, echoing in the small space.

"Harder," Sam begged. "Faster."

Elijah wasn't being gentle, but Sam seemed quite content with him pile driving into her, hard and fast. Just like she'd asked.

Logan watched Sam. He watched Elijah. He watched where they were joined, and his cock began to stir again. No, he didn't believe he was going to be up for anything anytime soon, but he knew before the night was out, he'd be inside of her.

Elijah's pace slowed, surprising Logan.

"One of these days," Elijah said, sounding as though he'd just run a mile, "we're both going to fuck you at the same time."

Logan's dick took notice of that. He didn't need to be a genius to know what Elijah was referring to since they'd already double penetrated her. He was referring to both of them in her pussy at once.

"Oh, God," Sam groaned.

"Do you want that, Sam? Do you want Logan and me to fuck you at the same time? To fill your pussy?"

Sam glanced over at him, and Logan's dick was now almost at full mast again. If she said yes, he wasn't sure he would need to wait until later that night.

"Yes," she said, her eyes meeting Logan's before sliding back to Elijah's face. "Right now. Fuck me, both of you. Please."

Elijah glanced over at Logan, his brows furrowed. It was almost as though Elijah was apologizing for bringing up the subject, knowing Logan had just come. He damn sure wasn't as young as he used to be, and getting hard this soon after generally didn't come easy for him.

But the idea of double stuffing Sam... Ahh, fuck.

Logan was already stroking his cock, the insatiable thing rock hard once more as he thought about sliding inside of Sam, alongside Elijah.

Granted, it wasn't happening in that swing.

Apparently, Elijah already knew that, because he was unstrapping Sam's ankles and her wrists, although he still penetrated her completely.

When he stood back up, Sam had wrapped her arms around his neck, and Elijah lifted her easily, carrying her over to the far wall, where he put his back against it.

"Fuck," Logan growled.

Not wasting time, Logan moved up to the pair, his chest pressing against Sam's back, his hands cupping her ass to assist Elijah in holding her. She couldn't wrap her legs around Elijah because he was using the wall as leverage, but with Logan's help, Sam was able to lean into Elijah.

Bending at the knees, he had to let go of Sam long enough to line up his cock.

*Fucking hell.*

He'd never done this before. Never had his cock touch another man's cock like this, but here he was, sliding into Sam slowly. Ever so fucking slowly. She was so fucking tight.

"Oh, fuck," Sam moaned. "It's too much."

Elijah didn't move, because he was holding most of Sam's weight, his cock buried inside of her.

"Do you want me to stop?" Logan asked, his breaths ragged as their combined heat on his dick pulled at that tiny thread of control he was holding on to.

"No," she said, but Logan wasn't quite sure he believed her.

"If it's too much, Sam, tell us."

Logan continued on his quest to join Elijah inside of Samantha, even slower this time, their cocks pressed tightly together within her snug, wet pussy.

"Fuck, baby," Logan groaned. "This feels good. Almost there."

Once Logan was inside of her as far as he could go, he didn't move. Neither did Elijah as they waited for her body to adjust to them both being inside of her.

At the same fucking time.

Logan was watching Sam's face, and when she leaned in to kiss Elijah, he knew she was relaxing somewhat. He continued to watch as the kiss heated, their mouths fumbling as they attempted to inhale one another, and only then did he start moving. Sam moaned, trying to grind down against them, but it was difficult to do in this position.

Note to self: *Next time, try this in a bed.*

"Ahh, fuck," Elijah groaned. "Your pussy's so tight, Sam. You're gonna make me come."

Logan picked up the pace, thrusting into her right alongside Elijah's cock.

Neither of them was wearing a condom, which made the sensation ... too fucking good.

"Oh, yes," Sam moaned. "More," she pleaded, "harder, Logan. I'm so close."

Logan adjusted his stance, giving himself more traction as he began to thrust into her relentlessly. A fine sheen of sweat coated his entire body, his clothes sticking to him as he fucked his wife while Elijah was buried inside of her.

She was double stuffed, and the thought had him barreling close to the edge once again.

"Faster," Elijah groaned. And Logan gave him what he asked for, ramming into her, unable to fully retreat, but enough so that the friction became intoxicating.

"Yes!" Sam bellowed. "God, yes! I'm coming!"

"Fuck!" Logan stilled as her muscles locked on to them both, milking him.

"Ahh!" Elijah groaned at the same time Logan's release ripped through him.

Several minutes later, with Sam back on her feet, they stood there trying to catch their breaths. Elijah was holding most of their combined weight because Logan was barely able to keep himself upright.

"That was a first," Sam finally said, breaking the silence.

Elijah glanced at Logan, his eyes reflecting his disbelief. "Really?"

"Yeah," Logan admitted as he tried to regulate his breathing.

"Well, hell."

"What?" Sam asked, shifting so she could look up at both of them.

"Nothing. I'm just wondering what other firsts we can look forward to."

"Don't worry, I'm sure there'll be plenty more," Sam suggested optimistically.

Yeah, Logan had absolutely no doubt about that.

# Epilogue

*Three months later...*

Elijah sat on the bed, glancing at the box sitting on the floor at his feet. He'd sliced open the tape a few seconds ago, but now he just needed a minute.

"Hey," Samantha greeted him, and Elijah looked up to see her standing in the doorway.

"Hey."

"What are you doing?" she asked, moving farther into the room.

"I was..." Elijah glanced down at the box, then back up at her. "I don't want to leave them in the box."

Sam reached down, pulling open one of the flaps to peer inside. She squatted down on her haunches beside the box and looked up at him.

Elijah had a difficult time looking at her at the moment.

"These are your pictures of Beth."

Yeah, they were. And they'd been sitting in that box for the last week, ever since he had moved. Well, technically, *they* had moved. It wasn't long after their night together at Devotion when they'd checked out that swing for the second time that they had decided to take their relationship to the next level. And that meant moving in together.

But apparently, somewhere along the way, Sam had found a house. Well, more like Sierra had found them a house, dangerously close to her own. After a lot of discussion, Logan had finally told them he was ready to move. He was quite impressed with the house they'd looked at, and he liked the concept of it becoming *their* house.

The three of them.

Not Logan's. Not Sam's. Not Elijah's.

Logan had felt it best to start anew.

So, they'd bought the house. Granted, the deed was in Logan's and Sam's names, but there was a contract that reflected Elijah's partial ownership.

And now they had a house. With two complete master bedrooms. Sam and Logan were in one, Elijah in the other, although there were plenty of nights when Sam would join him in his bed. Sometimes just for a little while, sometimes all night.

And of course, there was a third room, which they'd turned into a playroom. Fully equipped with, yes, another king-sized bed. That way, they could all sleep in the same room if they chose to. Oh, and a swing. They couldn't forget the swing.

So yes, this new house — new to them, anyway — was the perfect setup. At least it had been for the last week, since they'd officially moved in.

Hence, the reason Elijah was still unpacking.

"I was thinking..." Sam said, bringing Elijah's attention back to her. "We kind of set aside a place for these pictures. If you don't want them there, that's fine, but I thought you'd want to show them off. Beth's a part of you; therefore, she's a part of us."

Elijah just stared back at Sam, unsure what to say.

"Come here," she told him as she rose to her feet after taking one of the pictures from the box. When she took his hand, he relented and pushed to his feet.

He followed her into the living room, where Logan was sitting on the couch watching television. When they walked in, he grabbed the remote and shut it off. Sam led Elijah over to the set of floor-to-ceiling bookshelves that lined one wall while Logan came to his feet. The bookshelf was already filled with books, but there were several shelves that had been decorated with vases and trinkets, and yes, picture frames.

There were pictures of Logan and Sam's wedding, some of Sam's parents, Logan's parents, Logan's grandfather, and pictures of Luke, Sierra, Cole, and Hannah. He noticed a recent one of the three of them, taken by Sierra when they'd come to look at the house for the very first time. There were also several empty spaces, and Sam set Beth's picture in one of the spots.

"I made room for all of them," she told him now.

Elijah didn't know what to say. Sam must've realized he was a little choked up, because she walked right up to him and wrapped her arms around his waist. Elijah buried his face in her neck, holding on to her just as tightly.

Logan's hand rested on his shoulder again. Elijah had learned that was Logan's way of showing his support. Just a show of solidarity, letting him know that he was there.

"Thank you, Sam," he whispered long minutes later.

"I'm not sure what you're thanking me for, but you're welcome."

Elijah smiled at that, lifting his head and cupping her face in his hands. "Thank you for loving me. For knowing just what I need."

Sam smiled, too, as she glanced between the two of them. "Sometimes it takes more than one person to complete us. I've realized that now. The people who come into our lives affect us; they mold us into who we will become. Logan taught *me* what love is. And I'm grateful to Beth. Through her, *you* learned what love is. And *because* of them, we get to share a little bit of that love with each other."

Elijah stared into Sam's eyes; the emotion he saw there stole his breath. "It's more than a little, Sam. Definitely more than a little."

# ACKNOWLEDGMENTS

Samantha and Logan were the start of it all for me. I remember meeting Logan for the first time (in my head). He was the answer to all of Sam's innermost desires. He was strong, handsome, and utterly alpha. He could handle her at her best and at her worst. And she fell for him immediately, even if she had a hard time dealing with it at first.

And ever since Conviction (CD #1), I've felt as though Sam and Logan were still teetering on the edge of real, wholesome happiness although they had continued to tell me that was all in my head. But I hope you agree that Elijah has completed them. And in turn, they've completed him.

As always, I want to thank you, the reader, for taking a chance on me in the beginning and continuing to stay with me. This is an amazing journey and I'm so glad you're along for the ride!

# ABOUT NICOLE EDWARDS

*New York Times* and *USA Today* bestselling author Nicole Edwards lives in the suburbs of Austin, Texas with her husband and their youngest of three children. The two older ones have flown the coup, while the youngest is in high school. When Nicole is not writing about sexy alpha males and sassy, independent women, she can often be found with a book in hand or attempting to keep the dogs happy. You can find her hanging out on social media and interacting with her readers - even when she's supposed to be writing.

## CONNECT WITH NICOLE

I hope you're as eager to get the information as I am to give it. Any one of these things is worth signing up for, or feel free to sign up for all. I promise to keep each one unique and interesting.

**NIC NEWS:** If you haven't signed up for my newsletter and you want to get notifications regarding preorders, new releases, giveaways, sales, etc., then you'll want to sign up. I promise not to spam your email, just get you the most important updates.

**NICOLE'S HOT SHEET:** A couple of years ago I produced a weekly hot sheet that gave a summary of what I'd done and what I had in the works, and I have decided to bring it back. This is a more personal newsletter that I send out for those who are curious about me, my family, my dogs, and all that goes along with the daily author life.

**NICOLE'S BLOG:** My blog is used for writer ramblings, which I am known to do from time to time. I will keep these separate from the newsletter updates or what I post in the Hot Sheet so that I don't duplicate in your inbox.

**NICOLE NATION:** I created Nicole Nation on my website to provide exclusive content to my readers including, First Look notifications, sneak peeks, A Day in the Life character stories, exclusive giveaways, cards from Nicole, Join Nicole's review team. It's free and gets you access to exclusive content you won't find anywhere else!

**NN ON FACEBOOK:** Join my reader group to interact with other readers, ask me questions, play fun weekly games, celebrate during release week, and enter exclusive giveaways!

**INSTAGRAM:** Basically, Instagram is where I post pictures of my dogs, so if you want to see epic cuteness, you should follow me.

**TEXT:** Want a simple, fast way to get updates on new releases? Sign up for text messaging. If you are in the U.S. simply text NICOLE to 64600. I promise not to spam your phone. This is just my way of letting you know what's happening because I know you're busy, but if you're anything like me, you always have your phone on you.

| | |
|---|---|
| Website: | NicoleEdwardsAuthor.com |
| Facebook: | /Author.Nicole.Edwards |
| Instagram: | NicoleEdwardsAuthor |
| BookBub: | /NicoleEdwardsAuthor |

By Nicole Edwards

# The Walkers

**AUSTIN ARROWS**
Rush
Kaufman

**CLUB DESTINY**
Conviction
Temptation
Addicted
Seduction
Infatuation
Captivated
Devotion
Perception
Entrusted
Adored
Distraction

**DEAD HEAT RANCH**
Boots Optional
Betting on Grace
Overnight Love

**DEVIL'S BEND**
Chasing Dreams
Vanishing Dreams

**MISPLACED HALOS**
Protected in Darkness
Salvation in Darkness
Bound in Darkness

**OFFICE INTRIGUE**
Office Intrigue
Intrigued Out of The Office
Their Rebellious Submissive
Their Famous Dominant
Their Ruthless Sadist
Their Naughty Student
Their Fairy Princess
Owned

## PIER 70
Reckless
Fearless
Speechless
Harmless
Clueless

## SNIPER 1 SECURITY
Wait for Morning
Never Say Never
Tomorrow's Too Late

## SOUTHERN BOY MAFIA/DEVIL'S PLAYGROUND
Beautifully Brutal
Without Regret
Beautifully Loyal
Without Restraint

## STANDALONE NOVELS
Unhinged Trilogy
A Million Tiny Pieces
Inked on Paper
Bad Reputation
Bad Business

## NAUGHTY HOLIDAY EDITIONS
2015
2016